Jacob's Mob

C J Bessell

Other Books by C J Bessell

The Copper Road Series
Pioneers of Burra
For the Love of Family

Margaret

© Copyright C J Bessell 2021

ISBN: 978-0-6451051-0-0

This book is based on the life of my ancestor Aaron Price.

Chapter One

Wallis Plains, 1825, New South Wales

Aaron stood leaning against the railing as he waited. He rubbed his hands together and blew his warm breath on them; he could barely feel his fingers. Lawrie glanced towards the Overseer's house again and spat a wad of saliva into the dirt. Aaron gazed at the glob of saliva in distaste. He didn't think Lawrie even noticed he spat when he was agitated.

"How much longer is he gonna make us wait do yer think?" said Lawrie jutting his chin out in the direction of the house. "Must 'ave a real good job lined up for us."

Aaron nodded. "Aye, he'll want us to punish us for sure."

No doubt he'd saved a choice job for them. He knew they were good mates with Riley who'd they'd carted off for a flogging yesterday. He bet Wilkins would've liked to have had all three of them flogged for the four sheep that went missing.

5

Instead, Reid, the local Magistrate had only found Riley guilty. Fifty lashes for four sheep though - Aaron shuddered. Reid was well known for handing out harsh sentences. Wilkins wouldn't have been happy that he'd only sentenced Riley though, and he'd want to punish them somehow.

The other convicts had been assigned their work for the day and had already set off. He'd been keeping Aaron and Lawrie waiting for at least half an hour already. Aaron

shifted his weight and sighed. Shit, he'd had enough. He scowled bitterly at what had landed him in this God-forsaken place.

Not that he blamed his mate James Barton for it. No, he'd come to his own decision to rob Robinson's house, even though it had been James' idea, he couldn't lay blame there. And maybe if he'd stayed home that night and faced his father and his foul mood things would've turned out differently.

It was getting dark before he'd arrived home. His father was a stickler for punctuality, and he hoped he was running late as well. With any luck, he'd been delayed at the public house. Aaron entered the small house through the back door which led straight into the kitchen. His father and young brother were already seated at the table. His father cast a grim look in his direction, his upper lip curling into a snarl.

"What time do you call this boy?"

"Go wash up," said his mother over her shoulder. She was busy stirring dinner on the stove, while his sister Mary was getting the plates out of the dresser. Her soft brown eyes locked with his hazel ones for the briefest moment, but it was enough to tell him their father was in a foul temper.

"Sorry Pa," he said before heading straight back outside again to wash up. Damn. It wasn't going to be a pleasant evening. Maybe he ought to not go in for supper? He knew he'd be welcome at James', and his mother was a damn fine cook. He dried his hands and cast one last look towards the kitchen. The twinge of guilt he felt for leaving his mother and sister to take the brunt of his father's mood lasted no more than an instant. He headed off to

James Barton's house without giving them another thought.

Aaron had known James Barton for about as long as he could remember. He'd spent many hours at his house and was treated as one of the family by his mother Frances. His father George was a quiet God-fearing man; almost an exact opposite to Aaron's own.

He knocked on the door which was promptly opened by Frances Barton. She was rosy-cheeked with a warm and generous smile that went all the way to her pale blue eyes. She smiled warmly and gestured him into the house.

"We've started supper, but you know you're more'n welcome," she said leading him through to the kitchen. "Sit down. Sit."

She sat back down and continued eating the hearty stew she'd prepared. The pot was sitting in the middle of the table and Aaron sat down and scooped out a generous helping.

"Thank you."

The other family members at the table generally nodded and grunted in his direction. He took this to be the family's greeting and returned the gestures.

"So your old man's in a temper is he?" asked James grinning at him. "I don't know why you don't move out. Get your own place."

"You know I'm working on it," he replied spooning another mouthful of the delicious stew into his mouth. "Just as soon as I've got enough money I'll be out of there."

"Is that all that's stopping you?" said James eyeing him from across the table. "I'm sure we could easily fix that."

Aaron gave him a look that clearly said 'shut up'. He didn't want James' family alerted to their nefarious activities. He noticed his father was giving him a queer look and he groaned inwardly. James had such an odd sense of humour. He was obviously grinning in between shoving his supper into his mouth. Aaron was squirming and James knew it.

"Easy for some," said Aaron trying to ignore the odd look his mother was now casting his way. "I see you're still living at home then."

James grinned at him and shrugged.

"Have you not asked that lovely Skinner girl to marry you yet?" said Frances. "You know if you don't hurry up someone else will be askin' her."

"Aye," said James wiping his mouth with the back of his hand. "How would that be? You havin' just had her name tattooed on your arm."

"You ought not be wastin' your money on such things, Aaron," said George Barton from the head of the table. "Work hard and save your money so you can marry your sweetheart and get your own place."

"Aye, I will," promised Aaron reaching for another helping of stew.

He was thankful when the conversation moved on to general family matters. However, he wondered if James had a new escapade in mind. His earlier comment on how easy it would be to get some money had piqued his interest.

Up until now, their activities had been limited to a bit of pickpocketing and stealing liquor from the Talbot Inn. He would definitely be interested in doing something a bit bigger if James was up for it. The quicker he could get his hands on enough money the better. He couldn't wait to get out from under his father's nose and out on his own. Well, not quite on his own – with Nellie.

As soon as supper was done James gestured to him to follow him outside. The two settled down on the back wall of the garden. They were well out of earshot from the house and although it was a chilly night, Aaron didn't notice.

"Your Pa and Ma were looking at me so queer like," said Aaron giving James a shove. "You've got an odd sense of humour."

"You worry too much," said James with a laugh. "Anyways they haven't a clue."

Aaron grunted in reply.

"So I reckon we ought to do a bit of house breakin'," said James raising his eyebrows, "and I've got just the place picked out."

"Housebreaking?" said Aaron slightly aghast. He was up for something bigger, but this wasn't just bigger, it was a lot more dangerous. "You're mad. We'll hang if we get caught."

"Well we best not get caught then," replied James grinning. "You want to marry Nellie, don't you? We'd get enough money in one hit for you to move out of home."

The very mention of Nellie's name sent a tremor down his spine. God, he couldn't wait until he could ask for her hand. Then there was his father. Charles Price was an angry drunk who regularly terrorised and beat his wife and children. Aaron had been beaten more times than he cared to remember – no, he couldn't wait to get out of there. Maybe with enough money he could get them all out, including his mother who generally took the brunt of his father's temper.

"Come on what do you say?" said James impatiently bouncing his leg up and down. "I've got just the place picked out. I happen to know they're away for a few days. Somethin' about a family funeral."

"Alright, tell me," he replied looking at James' excited face. "I'm not saying I will though." Petty thieving was one thing, burglary quite another.

"You know ol' Robinson's place down in Clanfield? It's the stone joint on the corner."

"Aye, I know the one. You want to break into Robinson's house?" Aaron sucked in a deep breath. It was a plum choice. Old William Robinson was a smart dresser and always seemed to have plenty of money on him. Perhaps robbing his person would reap more than burglarising his house though.

"Aye. Can you imagine the stuff he'd have? Hats to start with. He's always wearin' a fine hat; he must have loads of 'em," said James jumping to his feet. "We'd be able to sell 'em real easy."

"Why don't we just rob him? It'd be easy to roll him one night when he's coming out of the public house." Aaron didn't think they'd hang for that either. "It wouldn't be half as risky."

"Where's your sense of adventure? Come on – let's do a burglary. I promise you, they're not home."

Hell, why not? James' excitement was contagious and Aaron heard himself agreeing with the plan.

Jacob's Mob

"Let's go drink on it while we work out the best time to break in," said James rubbing his hands together.

Aaron couldn't help but grin at him and nod in agreement.

~

Rustling in the scrub behind him made Aaron turn just in time to see a half crouched Patrick Riley emerge from the bushes. What the hell was he doing here? Riley glanced nervously left and right before standing up and approaching the two men.

"Is Wilkins in there?"

"What the fuck are yer doing here?" said Lawrie gawking at him.

"Sh," said Riley putting his finger to his pursed lips. "I escaped those idiots an' I've got us some rides. They're back there," he said indicating to the scrub behind them. "Do yer reckon we can take Wilkins?"

"And Jones," said Aaron grinning at him. "Aye, I reckon we can take them. What did you have in mind then?"

"Gettin' the hell outta this place afore they strip the skin off me back. What else?"

Aaron nodded. Fair enough. If they caught Riley now they'd be giving him more than fifty lashes. The very thought made his skin crawl and he shuddered.

"Yer don't have ter join me if yer don't want ter," said Riley looking at the other two men, his light grey eyes shining with determination. "I won't blame yer either way."

"I'm in," said Lawrie without a second's hesitation.

Aaron sucked in a deep. He saw no future in staying, but still, absconding was a serious offence. He'd arrived at Jacob's farm over a year ago, and it had been a year of exhausting hard labour. There was no hope of it ending any time soon – he'd been sent here for life.

"Aye," he replied resolutely.

They quickly came up with a plan to surprise the two inhabitants. Riley and Lawrie would rush the front door while Aaron went around through the back. They hoped to catch the two unawares. Aaron's heart was hammering as he snuck down the side of the house to the back door. He stepped cautiously onto the porch and waited; poised ready to shove the door open a second after the others went in the front. Every muscle was tensed tight and he pressed his lips together as he breathed in heavily through his nose. He could feel the adrenalin thrumming through his veins and it was exhilarating.

As soon as he heard the front door smash open and Lawrie yell like a banshee he rushed inside. Riley was already wrestling Wilkins to the ground and appeared to have the situation in hand. Lawrie, on the other hand, was circling Jones, his hands outstretched. Aaron rushed forward and grabbed Jones from behind. He wrapped his arms around his middle and shoved his shoulder as hard as he could into his kidneys. He made an awful oomph sound and went sprawling on the floor with Aaron landing on top of him.

They had the two men subdued in no time. They tied their hands and feet before dragging them out onto the veranda and securing them to a post. Lawrie waved a knife under Wilkins's nose and threatened to run him through if he so much as breathed too loud. He glared back at Lawrie with his good eye. His left one was already half-closed and showing signs of bruising where Riley had hit him.

"Let's git what we can an' git outta here," said Riley wiping away a trickle of blood that was oozing from his nose.

The three men went back into the house and began searching the place for supplies and anything of any use. The Overseer's house wasn't well stocked with provisions, but they took all there was. This amounted to not much more than some salt pork and a sack of turnips along with tea and sugar. A small bag of flour and some hard biscuits rounded out their haul.

They took the two muskets with the shot as well as a few cooking utensils and a sabre. Aaron grabbed the two water canteens that were sitting on the table and slung them over his shoulder. They'd obviously been filled ready for the day. Lawrie had several blankets tossed over his arm. Good. It was the middle of bloody winter they were going to need them.

The three men stepped out onto the front veranda and looked cautiously around the yard. There was no sign of anyone. Their two prisoners were still firmly secured to the veranda post. Riley gave Wilkins a kick in the ribs as he went by.

"That's for bein' such a bastard."

They hurried across the yard and into the scrub to the place where Riley had tied the horses. There were three of them and they quickly tied their blankets and provisions to one and Riley and Lawrie mounted up without delay. They looked at Aaron who was still standing there staring at the horses in trepidation.

"Come on man," said Riley expertly turning his mount and holding out his hand.

"Aye," said Aaron eyeing the animal in front of him. He swallowed as he tried to imagine how he was going to get on the beast.

Riley and Lawrie were both farmers of a sort. Riley had been a shepherd back in Ireland, and Lawrie a ploughman. They knew their way around animals. Aaron didn't. He'd been a stonemason back in

Oxford and although he'd gotten used to sheep, he'd never ridden a horse in his life.

"Just throw yer leg over an' hang on," suggested Riley grinning at him. He knew Aaron didn't have a clue how to ride. When he'd gone to Reid's to steal the mounts he'd considered taking one for each of them but changed his mind. Now would not be a good time for Price to learn to ride.

"Aye," said Aaron again. He took a deep breath and grabbing hold of Riley's outstretched hand swung up behind him. Shit, it was a long way up. He wrapped his arms around Riley's lean stomach and hung on for dear life.

"No need ter squeeze the life outta me," he said laughing.

He heard Lawrie chuckling behind him as they turned the horses and headed off. It was slow going through most of Jacob's land which was uncleared bush. They skirted around a large swamp by the river and headed north. Aaron had no idea where they were going, and he doubted his companions did either. The horses picked their way through the thick undergrowth with no discernible tracks or pathways, and

Aaron began to relax his grip on Riley. At this pace there was no fear he was going to fall off.

The bush gave way to more open land as they headed uphill from the river. Misty rain began falling which was proving to be more of a nuisance than anything. Aaron pulled his hat down lower and stuck his face into Riley's back. A few minutes later Lawrie came alongside dragging the packhorse behind him.

"I reckon we ought ter head for higher ground," he said looking ahead up the hill. "We'll want ter be able to see 'em if they come after us."

"Oh they'll be comin' after us for sure," said Riley nodding.

"Aye. We'll need a lookout and shelter as well," said Aaron poking his head up. "Any idea how far we've come?"

"Five or six miles I'd say," said Riley twisting in the saddle. "We'll need ter put a bit more distance between us an' them if we can."

"Aye. Let's go," said Lawrie urging his mount forward.

They continued on for several more miles, heading upwards to the top of the hill. The area was thickly treed with wattles and gums which provided some protection from the wind and rain. However, there were no caves or other natural shelters they could use. Lawrie came to a halt by a rocky outcrop. It would provide some shelter and would protect their backs from unnoticed intruders.

Aaron slid off the back of the horse with eagerness. He was stiff and sore from so many hours on the beast. He rubbed his backside cautiously. He was sure he had a blister between his arse cheeks. As far as he was concerned the day he got back on a horse would be a day too soon.

~

Chapter Two

Vicars Jacob's Farm, 1825

Dan Wilkins was livid. He ripped off the last of the ropes that had secured him to the veranda for the past two hours. Shit! He untied Jones before the two headed into the house.

"The bastards have taken everythin'," said Dan looking around the ransacked cottage. The first thing he noticed was that the muskets were gone and he groaned as he ran his hands through his hair. Shit, the buggers were armed. Jacob's didn't pay him enough money to track down armed absconders – they were going to need help.

"What we gonna do?" asked Alex Jones as he peered around the room. "I don't know 'bout trackin' runaways."

Dan ran his hands through his dirty blonde hair again. It would take days to get word to Jacob's. He was tending to business down in Sydney and wasn't likely to be visiting any time soon. He'd need to send word to him of course, but the other settlers would also need to know they had croppies on the loose. Armed croppies, he corrected himself. Shit!

The nearest neighbour was Donald McLeod. He owned the lot south of them on the bend in the river and Dan was pretty sure he'd be home. Even if he wasn't able to help track them himself, Dan thought he'd raise a search party. At least he hoped so.

"Come on," said Dan rushing out the door. "We'll notify McLeod. He'll know what to do."

Dan got the feeling Alex didn't care as long as he wasn't being asked to go out after the runaways himself. If he was honest, he didn't blame him. He had no intention of joining a search party either. Of course, he was Jacob's Overseer; he'd need to stay here to keep the rest of them buggers in line.

The two headed off to raise the alarm. Dan knew the men had a good couple of hour's head start on any pursuers, and he wasn't sure if they were on foot or not. He really should have paid more attention, but he was so furious at being hogtied to the veranda that he hadn't thought of anything else.

By the time they got to McLeod's, it was starting to rain and Dan was panting and gasping for air. He had a stitch in his side from running almost nonstop. He rubbed the annoying pain in his side as he stepped onto the front verandah and hammered on the door.

It was opened a minute later by Donald McLeod who raised his eyebrows at the state of Wilkins but invited them inside. He had a mug of coffee in one hand and he told his cook to pour some for their guests.

"Thank ye," said Dan brushing the offer aside. "We come with grave news. Three of Jacob's croppies have absconded an' they're armed. We came as soon as we could." He was still panting, and he doubled over as he tried to catch his breath and ease the pain in his side.

McLeod spluttered on a mouthful of coffee and stared at the two men. "What! When did this happen?"

"A few hours ago I'm afraid," replied Dan standing up and looking McLeod in the eye. "They caught us unawares an' the bastards tied us up an' stole muskets an' other things."

"I suppose Vic's in Sydney?"

"Aye."

"Well best send him word of it, but we can't wait for him to get here," said McLeod gulping down the last of his coffee. "I'll arrange a search party. Any idea which way they went?"

"No," replied Dan looking shamefaced. "I don't even know if they were on foot or no."

"No worry. I'll take it from here. You best get back and keep a close eye on the rest of them. If I were you I'd get them mustered. No telling if more of them will get stupid ideas into their heads and run off."

Dan nodded in agreement before heading for the door. The last thing he needed was more of them to run. Shit, that would be the last straw. He nudged Jones who was waiting on the veranda, and the two headed back to Jacob's.

~

As soon as the two men left Don McLeod raised the alarm with his Overseer George McIntire. "We're going to need trackers," he said scratching his head. "No telling which way they've gone. Ride over to James Reid's and see if any of the natives can be coerced into helping out. He generally has an idea where they are."

"Aye sir," he replied over his shoulder as he headed for the stables.

In the meantime, Don grabbed firearms and armed two of his men. It would be wise to be on alert. There was no way of knowing if the runaways had got as far away as they could, or if they intended to attack nearby settlers. Don wasn't taking any chances.

George McIntire returned an hour later with two native trackers in tow. He also had news that the runaways had stolen Reid's horses the previous night. So they were not only armed but on horseback. They could be anywhere. Don was glad the natives had joined the pursuit. They'd have no hope of catching them otherwise.

A small search party was quickly assembled. It consisted of Don McLeod, along with his Overseer George McIntire and another of his men. They were all armed and mounted and being guided by two experienced native trackers. They'd lost precious hours, but Don was confident they'd be able to catch them up as long as the light held.

They immediately headed over to Vicars Jacob's farm to pick up the trail. The two natives had no trouble finding the trail left by the horses, and they immediately headed north. They kept up a good pace to start with as the hoof prints were still visible in the soft earth, even Don could've followed the trail. As the land started to rise though the tracks became less obvious and the trackers looked for other clues.

They picked their way uphill from the river for several miles constantly keeping an eye out for any sign of them. They stopped by a small creek to water the horses and have a bite to eat. It was already mid-afternoon and Don's confidence was wavering. He was surprised they hadn't caught up to them already.

They continued for another hour or so to the top of the hill where the trackers came to an abrupt halt. Through the trees, they pointed to several horses. They were hobbled and nibbling on the grass under the shelter of a rocky outcrop. The men quickly dismounted and took cover behind a stand of lilly pilly. They were tall and bushy and offered an excellent hiding spot from which they could survey the area without being seen. Don's heart was hammering in his chest but all around the bush was silent. After a few minutes of checking the area, they realised the horses were alone. Don wondered briefly why they would've abandoned them.

"Dey went that way," said Mullabuy indicating that the runaways had gone east from here.

They secured Reid's horses before continuing to track the runaways. The trail headed back down the hill and they followed it for as long as they could. The dwindling light forced them to call off the search and head back, much to Don's disappointment. They delivered the horses back to James Reid on the way and appraised him of the situation.

"Thank you for returning my horses," he said to McLeod. "I'm sorry you didn't catch them. That Patrick Riley's a real bad one. I'll speak with Alexander Scott in the morning about getting some soldiers out to pursue them."

"Aye that's a good idea," replied Don mounting his horse. "In the meantime, we all need to be on high alert. No telling what they're planning."

~

Aaron yawned and wrapped the woollen blanket more firmly around his shoulders. It had been a cold and uncomfortable night. They hadn't dared light a fire; anyway, there was no dry kindling around to light it with. They'd found a partially sheltered spot with an overhanging rock to sleep under, which had provided some protection from the steady rain.

Aaron stood up and stretched. His muscles were sore and tight, no doubt from hours on the back of that damn horse yesterday. He hoped he wouldn't have to do that again.

"So what's the plan," said Lawrie munching on a hard biscuit. "We're gonna need more supplies that's for sure."

"Aye," replied Riley. "Don't worry we'll git more supplies, but we've got more important business ter attend ter first."

Lawrie raised his eyebrows quizzically at him, but Aaron thought he knew what he was on about. Revenge - pure and simple. He didn't blame him. He thought he'd feel the same and given the opportunity would act on it. James Reid was well known for being a tough authoritarian Magistrate. He handed out tougher penalties for minor misdemeanours than any of the other Magistrates in the area. Aaron thought fifty lashes with the cat for losing sight of four stupid sheep that would probably make their way back to the flock by morning, was a gross over punishment.

"Reid the bastard of course," said Riley getting to his feet. "I'd like to see how he feels as I strip the flesh of his back."

Lawrie swallowed his biscuit and got to his feet as well. "I'd pay good money ter see that."

"If you had any," quipped Aaron.

"Well let's do it then," said Riley grinning at them. "We'll need another musket or two. I don't reckon we can be too far from Harris' farm. We ought ter be able git weapons there. An' if we're lucky we might git breakfast as well."

Lawrie was all for a free meal. They gathered their weapons and headed back to where they'd hobbled the horses late yesterday. Lawrie was disappointed to discover they weren't where they'd left them. Aaron, on the other hand, sighed with relief. He'd been dreading getting back on the back of that beast today.

"It's probably for the best," said Riley looking around. "Horses are too easy ter track, an' I reckon they must've had native trackers out after us for them ter git this far."

Aaron agreed. The soft earth showed signs of numerous horses and men. They would need to be more careful if they hoped to stay ahead of any pursuit. Three men on foot would leave far less of a trail for the trackers to follow.

They headed south from the top of the hill and skirted around Graham's land. They could hear gangs of men working and had no desire to attract attention. Their best strategy lay in surprise. Standish Harris had a good-sized property north of the river. He wouldn't likely be there, but Riley was sure he had an Overseer who could be persuaded to part with weapons.

It was only a small cabin with about an acre of cleared land around it. There were several smaller outbuildings and as far as Riley could recall he only had half a dozen or so convicts. The three men sheltered behind a small outcrop of flowering gums and surveyed the scene. All was quiet; it could be that the hut was deserted, in which case it would be easy to break in and take what they wanted.

They'd just about convinced themselves of this when the back door opened and a tall thin man exited the hut. He headed down to the privy. Riley grinned and gestured to Lawrie and Aaron that they should surprise the man on his return. They hurried across the yard to the back porch and went inside.

It was a small cramped slab hut which consisted of one room. A single narrow bed was against one wall along with a table and chairs. A shabby dresser and a mouldy looking rug on the floor completed the furnishings. It smelled like burnt porridge. But burnt or not Lawrie helped himself to some straight out of the pot on the back of the woodstove.

"Yer want some?" he said stuffing a spoonful into his mouth. "It's not too bad."

"Aye," said Aaron.

They helped themselves to the Overseer's breakfast, all the while keeping a close eye on the back door. They needed to be ready to pounce on him as soon as he came back from the privy. Aaron opened the cupboards in the dresser and searched it. Apart from a bit of mouldy bread and some hardtack which he shoved into his pocket, it didn't contain much food that would be of use to them. He took a small sack of oats and left it at that. He rummaged through the drawers and found a hunting knife, a length of rope and a battered hip flask.

The back door swung open and Riley immediately stepped forward his loaded musket pointing directly at the man's head. "Mornin'," he drawled.

The surprise on the man's face was evident. However, he recovered quickly as he glanced around his small hut. "What the hell?"

"Put your hand's where we can see 'em," said Lawrie spooning the last of the burnt porridge into his mouth.

The man obliged, and Aaron quickly tied his hands behind his back and shoved him into a wooden chair. He secured him to the chair with another length of rope.

Riley relaxed and swung the musket over his shoulder. "Yer could save us the trouble of searchin' an' tell us where yer keep yer weapons an' ammunition."

Several thoughts flashed across the man's face before it settled on resignation. "In the chest under the bed," he said indicating with his chin to the end of the bedstead.

Aaron knelt down and peered under the bed. He pulled out a medium-sized wooden chest that was battered and had seen better days.

"Nice," he said as he opened it.

There were three pistols, two muskets and a good supply of ammunition. He took the lot and handed them out to Lawrie and Riley, keeping one of the pistols for himself. He shoved the last of the ammunition in his pocket and pushed the chest back under the bed.

"I reckon we ought to have enough to take Reid. What do you say?" said Aaron shoving the door open.

Riley grinned at him over his shoulder as he departed the cabin. "Aye, let's go git him."

~

Chapter Three

Wallis Plains, 1825

James Reid's property lay northeast of Jacob's farm on a sweeping bend of the river. It was well wooded from the north and the three men approached the main house using the natural cover of the bush. There was a cold wind blowing but Aaron was thankful the rain had eased and blue patches of sky were showing through the scudding clouds. He thought it must be getting on to noon, which meant Reid wouldn't be far away. If he wasn't already at home for his midday meal he'd be arriving soon.

The house was surrounded by a wide-open yard with a large barn and field of wheat to one side. Anyone approaching the front of the house would be easily seen by the occupants long before they reached the veranda. Riley was cautious. They were not likely to take Reid unawares. He would be well apprised of the situation and probably on the alert.

Aaron's heart was hammering in his chest as they waited; crouching behind the sprawling grevillea bushes.

"Do yer reckon he's in there?" said Lawrie turning his head and spitting.

Riley shook his head. "I dunno, but I reckon we'll soon find out." He crept forward craning for a better view. "There's naught for it. We'll just have ter run for it an' hope for the best. What do yer say?"

Lawrie was quick to agree, which made Aaron wonder if he'd do whatever Riley suggested, no matter how crazy. He suspected Lawrie was a bit in awe of Riley. Aaron reached out and put his hand on Riley's forearm. He paused and looked at him.

"Perhaps we ought to wait a bit longer."

"I hate the waitin'," said Riley and without waiting for a response he broke cover and started running across the yard. Lawrie was a split second behind him. Aaron groaned and started to follow the pair heedless of the danger.

A shot rang out – loud and close as it clipped the dirt at Riley's feet. It was quickly followed by another and the three men dived back under the cover of the grevilleas. Aaron's insides clenched in fear at the first shot and he felt his belly squirm horribly. He lay panting in the mud for a moment before scrambling up onto his knees.

Three men had emerged from the house and were crouched down low on the veranda. Aaron could see Reid's pale blonde head among them. Two more shots were fired, but they all knew there was little likelihood of them being hit at that distance. The threat, however, was unmistakable.

"I say we leave it for another day," said Aaron surveying the scene.

He could see Riley was reluctant, but he finally turned and nodded. "Aye. Yer right, there'll be another day for Reid."

The three quietly retreated from Reid's property and headed southwest back towards Jacob's farm. They were passing a small clump of acacia trees when someone yelled out.

"Oi."

Aaron froze and stepped into the shadows, peering through the foliage to see who had called to them. Riley had his musket primed and pointing in the general direction. Aaron thought he looked nervous as he scanned the bush for any signs of the man.

"Don't shoot," came the voice. "It's me...Paddy."

A moment later Paddy Clinch stepped into the clearing in front of the trees. He had one hand raised in surrender as he approached. A wide grin came across his face as the three emerged from behind the clump of trees and greeted him.

"I've been looking fer yer lads everywhere," he said grinning stupidly at them. "I ran off early this morning afore muster an' I've been hoping ter find yer." He raised the bag he was carrying. "I took all the provisions I could carry."

Lawrie let out a whoop of delight at that news. "All I've 'ad today is some burnt porridge an' a bit of 'ardtack," he said clapping him on the back. "You're a sight for sore eyes."

Aaron approached him with caution. He wasn't sure he completely trusted Paddy. His smiling freckled face belied the fact that the man had virtually no scruples. Aaron had steered clear of him as he had a nasty reputation. Still, he was obviously a good mate with Riley and Lawrie and so he extended the hand of friendship, but he wouldn't turn his back on him.

"So what's the plan?" said Paddy looking around at them.

"We're headin' back ter camp," said Riley grinning at him. "I thought yer might cook us some supper an' then we can talk about it."

"Awright," said Paddy slinging the bag over his shoulder. "I've got some nice pork in here that I'll turn into a stew fer yer."

Lawrie put his arm around his shoulders as they headed off for their camp. Paddy was well known for his cooking, and Lawrie obviously couldn't wait for supper. They gathered what dry kindling and wood as they could on the way back to camp. A brisk cold wind had been blowing most of the day which had helped to dry things out considerably.

Aaron dropped the pile of twigs and wood he'd collected with the others. There was enough wood for Paddy to cook supper, but not enough to burn all night. It would no doubt be another cold and uncomfortable night. Aaron didn't care. For the first time in more than two years he was a free man, and no matter how long that lasted he intended to enjoy it.

It didn't take long before they had a small fire going and Paddy had supper underway. Aaron had to concede that while Paddy might be a bit of a powder keg, he could certainly cook. He scooped another mouthful of the stew into his mouth and sighed. It was amazing how much better he felt on a full stomach.

"I reckon we've got the advantage," said Paddy sopping up his stew with a piece of bread. "They're outnumbered. I know fer a fact that all the lads will help us if they can. Shit, I reckon most of them would like ter join us."

"Really?" said Riley, the surprise evident on his face.

"Oh aye," said Paddy waving his bread around. "When we heard how you'd got the better of Wilkins we was all sorry we weren't there ter see it. An' half the lads

41

were for running off into the bush ter join in the fun."

"It was good ter give Wilkins what for," said Lawrie with a laugh. "But I don't know if they're outnumbered."

"Oh, sure they are. Come on, most of the landholders have got themselves an' their family. Maybe an Overseer an' another one or two men they can trust - then there's us. Each one's probably got about twenty of us, an' those lads are on our side."

Aaron didn't say much but he thought Paddy might be right. Given the choice, the convicts wouldn't support their masters. Many of them had been flogged or worked to the bone, and none of them owed anything to the settlers. Perhaps they could even make it worth their while to help them.

"What if we went in for a bit more stealing," said Aaron swallowing the last mouthful of stew. "We could trade that stuff with the croppies for information and such."

"Aye good idea," said Riley sitting back on his haunches. "The longer we can stay ahead of any pursuit the better. An' I want them buggers ter pay."

"Oh we'll make 'em pay," said Lawrie vehemently stuffing the last morsel of bread into his mouth.

~

The small smoky fire had burnt itself out sometime during the night, and Aaron woke feeling cold and stiff. The last time he'd felt this cold was in the old Castle Gaol in Oxford. He and James had been taken there a couple of days after they'd been caught burglarising Robinson's house.

He thought they'd only been in prison for about a week, but already he was losing track of time. He also knew that he'd be dead if it wasn't for George and Frances Barton. They'd come with food and warm clothes for both James and himself and had promised to come again. They'd paid the gaoler for James' food and lodgings, and he suspected they'd paid for him as well.

He shivered as he pulled the thin blanket closer about himself. The stone walls of the old castle were damp and bone numbingly cold. Even the air was frigid as every breath formed a cloud of mist in front of him. He could feel the cold icy fingers of the place seeping into his bones. He huddled closer to James seeking any extra warmth he could.

It wasn't the cold however that was bothering him. It was that his family had deserted him. At first, he'd just thought they didn't know where he was. Well, how could they? After they'd been caught that night the Watch had taken them to the Watch House. A day or so later they'd been stuffed into the back of a cart and brought here to the Castle Prison. That was a good fifteen miles or more from Bampton. Still, he thought his mother would've come; but she hadn't.

He'd brushed it off when James had talked about his family. He'd told him he didn't care or expect them to come, but privately he admitted it bothered him. He would likely never see his mother again. The longer time went on the less likely it became that she would come. He still hoped his sister Mary might come. He wanted very much to see someone that he loved before he died. He was pretty sure that was going to happen. The penalty for burglary was hanging. He swallowed and tried to bury the fear that rose from his belly like a writhing serpent.

He raised his head as he heard the jangle of keys and several whispered voices. In the glow of a lantern, he saw the gaoler accompanied by several people. Hope swelled in his breast for a moment thinking it might be someone to see him. Maybe his mother had come at last.

The rush of hope and warmth that came with it lasted a mere second. The gaoler continued passed their cell with the visitors in tow. He sighed and went back to his morose contemplation of his predicament.

Days went by. At least he thought so. The gaoler had come to inform him and James that their trial had been set for Wednesday. Apparently, that was two days away. He'd lost all hope of seeing his family again, and he hadn't dared even think about Nellie. That thought was just too painful. That was until this morning.

He heard the gaoler coming, but like James had kept his head buried under his blanket. It wasn't likely he'd be coming to their cell. It wasn't until he heard the key grating in the lock that he looked up.

"I'll give ye ten minutes," said the gaoler swinging open the cell door.

"Fifteen," said George Barton pressing a coin into the man's dirty palm. "And you'll leave the lantern."

He grunted but obliged.

James jumped to his feet to embrace his mother who came bustling into the cell behind George. He almost disappeared beneath her warm cloak which she wrapped around him along with her arms.

"Are you alright?" she said finally pulling from his embrace and peering at him.

"Aye."

"We've brought someone to see you too Aaron," said George gently pushing Nellie in front of himself so Aaron could see her.

The gaoler shut the door and locked it before shuffling off down the corridor without another word.

Aaron gaped at her for a moment before he could believe what his eyes were seeing. Tears welled in his eyes as he just stared at her.

"Nellie," he breathed trying to take all of her in.

She smiled weakly and took a nervous step towards him. "Aaron."

He saw the tears welling in her eyes as she stepped into his open arms. They stood there clinging to one another for what seemed to Aaron to be an interminable amount of time. She felt warm and solid in his arms, and he breathed in the scent of her. She smelled like freshly cut rose blossoms, sweet and heady.

He pushed her gently from him but didn't let her go. He couldn't let her go, but he wanted to look at her. He sucked in a cold breath and slowly breathed it out through his nose.

"I'm sorry," he finally said hugging her close again. "You must forget about me, Nellie. Go on with your life, find someone else." It broke his heart to say the words, but he wanted her to be free. To be free of him and any guilt that may come because of him.

"Tis not over yet," she said pulling out of his arms. "You might not be hanged."

Her blue eyes looked into his hazel ones with a ferocity that he'd not seen before. "I'm not giving up so easily, and you shouldn't either."

"Aye," he replied weakly. He didn't want to spend what precious time they had arguing.

He bent his head and kissed her softly. She responded by hugging him close and urging him to kiss her more passionately. They kissed and clung to one another knowing this would likely be the last time. They were completely oblivious to the other occupants in the small cell. After several minutes they separated but couldn't bear to not be touching. They stood together their fingers intertwined.

Time was running out. The gaoler would be returning in a few minutes and Aaron still hadn't asked about his family. Apart from seeing Nellie, which he still couldn't believe – he needed to know. Were they coming?

"Have you seen my mother?" he asked her tentatively.

"Aye I have," she replied casting her long lashes down over her eyes. "But only briefly."

He wasn't sure what that meant. "Do you know if they're coming to see me? Do they know I'm here?"

George Barton patted him on the arm. "Don't fuss yourself, lad."

"I need to know," he said taking in a deep breath and sighing. "Please, Nellie. What did she say?"

George cast a sideways look at Nellie. "I'll tell him if you like."

Nellie licked her lips and nodded.

"I'm afraid she's not coming," said George placing his arm around Aaron's shoulders. "Your father's forbidden her."

"Is that true?"

Nellie looked at him nervously. "Aye. I'm ever so sorry."

Aaron felt like the wind had been knocked out of him. Forbidden? He knew she would never disobey his father. He'd beat her senseless if she did. He groaned.

"What about Mary?"

"The same I'm afraid," said George looking solemn. "I hate to tell you the whole of it, but it seems I must."

Aaron stared at him. He had a crawling feeling in his gut which was slowly making its way outward. It crawled across his skin like a living thing. He shivered and gestured to George to get on with it.

"I'm afraid your fathers disowned you and forbidden anyone to even mention your name," said George hanging his head. "I don't know how he can do it, but he has."

He should have seen it coming. He should have known he'd turn his back on him. And yet, it hit him like a sledgehammer. His father no longer cared if he lived or died. Well, that was that then. He would get no help from that quarter. He swallowed the bitter bile and nodded. He was afraid if he tried to speak he'd lose all control.

A few minutes later the gaoler returned and unlocked the cell.

"Times up," he said gruffly standing back so they could leave.

"We'll be there on Wednesday," said George giving his son a final hug and pat on the shoulder. "You're both in our prayers."

Nellie clung to Aaron until the last possible second. "I'll try and be there as well."

"No don't," he said letting her go. "I couldn't bear it."

A moment later they were hustled out by the gaoler and their cell door clanged shut behind them. Aaron watched them go. He should've felt uplifted at seeing Nellie, but he didn't. His father's betrayal had left an open wound that he feared would never heal.

~

Chapter Four

late July 1825

The day was cold and overcast with an icy squall blowing. The men huddled under their blankets at the back of the rocky overhang where they got some respite from the chilly wind. Aaron held the mug of hot tea between his hands to warm his frozen fingers. He wondered if they should've perhaps chosen a better time of year than this to go bush. He shrugged. What was he complaining about?

He'd just spent the last year and a half working on Jacob's farm for no reward or money whatsoever. When he'd first arrived in Sydney he'd had no idea what the life of a convict would actually entail. He thought it would be similar to the last six months that he'd just spent on the hulk moored at Portsmouth.

Aaron and James became accustomed to the daily routine of life on board the hulk far quicker than Aaron would've imagined. Up at five in the morning and stow the hammocks, wash and dress for the day, clean the ward and deck before breakfast in the mess. Breakfast usually consisted of some dry bread and a pint of cocoa.

By seven-thirty, they were mustered and rowed ashore to work for the morning. They were kept busy loading or unloading timber and ballast from the ships. Sometimes they were moving rubble or shovelling dirt. At midday, they returned to the hulk for dinner before being rowed ashore again for the afternoon. Their working day finally finished at about half-past five. They had time for a quick wash before supper on the lower deck. This was usually a broth with potatoes and hard biscuit.

After supper, they were all required to attend evening prayer and for those that wanted they could learn to read and write. By the time prayers were done Aaron was so weary that he just hung his hammock and went to sleep.

After a few weeks, it all started to blend together. The monotony of work, eat and sleep was all there was to life. If Aaron hadn't been so bone-weary at the end of the day he might've had thoughts of escape. Of course, they were always guarded, particularly when they were working at the docks. He very much would've liked to have some alone time, just to go and sit by a river and be by himself. He'd even started dreaming of the solitude.

He sighed, closed his eyes and tried to go to sleep. All around him he could hear men already snoring, and he wished he could sleep. He wasn't sure how long he'd been on the hulk, or when they might be put on a transport to Botany Bay. Those thoughts were really consuming him. Where would they send him? He'd heard stories about Van Dieman's Land, and none of them were good. From what he understood the whole place was a penal settlement - men worked in chain gangs and were constantly flogged.

He swallowed and tried to put those thoughts out of his head. He and James had so far managed to avoid being flogged, but he thought it was just a matter of time. The least misdemeanour resulted in a flogging.

Argue with the Captain of their Ward, - flogging. Not working hard enough – flogging. Steal extra food, neglect of duty, not stowing your hammock; anything that strayed from the strict order of life and you'd find yourself stretched out over an oak barrel on the quarter deck. Twenty-five lashes with the cat was the general order. It made his skin crawl just to think of it and a shudder went through him.

He must've gone to sleep from sheer exhaustion because the next thing it was morning and he was being roused to get up. He rolled up his hammock and stowed it before going down to the lower deck to wash. Breakfast was a silent affair; no one was permitted to speak. Aaron sat down and waited for the messmen to fill his can with cocoa. Today didn't appear to be any different from any other day, but Aaron got the feeling something was afoot. He glanced at James, but he just sat staring ahead as he chewed his bread.

He shrugged and ate his breakfast. Whatever this odd feeling with the men was he presumed he'd find out soon enough. After breakfast, he expected to be mustered as usual and put in a work gang for the day. Instead, he was directed to the quarter-deck, along with James and sixty other prisoners. As soon as he stepped out onto the deck he realised what was going on. Another ship was tied up to the hulk with a gangplank between the two vessels – they were being transported today.

The Chaplain was already there waiting and he addressed them with kindness and beseeched them all to reform. He pointed out the punishment that lay ahead if they committed further crimes.

"By hard work and endeavour you will secure the full rights of a free man in your new country," he said looking at them all earnestly. "Discard your wicked ways and take this great opportunity."

He bowed his head and prayed. Aaron followed suit as did every man present. When the prayer ended the Captain of the York stepped forward.

"You'll be mustered and inspected by the Surgeon before boarding the Guildford," he said in his booming voice. "I expect you all to behave in an orderly fashion."

As each man's number was read out
he went forward for the Surgeon to inspect.
Soldiers from the Guildford waited at each
end of the gangplank. They would be
escorting them board and into the hold.

"Four oh forty seven."

Aaron stepped forward. The Surgeon
looked him up and down, asked him if his
lungs were clear and then gave him a nod.
One of the soldiers urged him forward down
the gangplank to the waiting ship. James
was ahead of him and he glanced around at
him with a look of relief on his face. The
day of departure had finally arrived and
Aaron greeted it with mixed feelings.

He knew he'd never see his family
again, and already the image of his mother
was fading. He could recall Nellie with ease
but shied away from doing so. Dwelling on
the past and what could not be changed only
increased his misery. He tried to turn his
thoughts to what might lie ahead. The
journey would not likely be a pleasant one,
but he hoped that it would at least be swift.
He knew he'd simply have to endure it.
Then what? He had no idea what awaited
him in the colonies.

Well, he knew now. After enduring more than a year as an assigned convict he knew exactly what to expect. Up at sunup with long days hauling timber, digging stumps or herding stupid sheep. Being told when to eat, when to sleep and what to do every hour of the day with no respite in sight. Anything, including the cold weather, was better than that. He sighed as he sipped his tea. It was black and sweet, and he felt it warm him. He breathed in the cold crisp air of being free.

They'd spent several days at their campsite and after much discussion had decided it was time to move. It wasn't wise to stay in one place for too long. They would find a new place to camp and then raid Maziere's farm on the western side of the river from Jacob's. Paddy thought he only had two men and half a dozen convicts, and he was rarely at the property.

By evening they'd cross back and attack Lieutenant Hick's. His property lay directly south of James Reid's. Riley hoped to instil fear into Reid by raiding his closest neighbour. He wanted him to be on guard and hoped to increase any anxiety that he might already be feeling.

By midday, they'd found a new campsite on Nowland's property near the creek. The area was heavily treed with acacias and gums and had a shallow muddy cave. Aaron wasn't sure that it was a cave as such, but rather part of the creek bank that had collapsed. Either way, it would provide good shelter from the wind and rain. They packed their provisions, blankets and other items at the back out of the weather, along with a good supply of dry firewood.

They raided Maziere's Overseer's cottage with ease and took all his provisions and weapons. They were all now well armed with muskets and pistols as well as a blunderbuss. As they were heading east across the river Paddy stopped abruptly. He pointed to where a convict was crouching under some callistemon shrubs. Riley and Paddy had their weapons aimed at the man before he'd even noticed them.

"What yer doing?" said Paddy holding his musket steady, pointing at the man's head.

The young man looked up in surprise but immediately raised his hands above his head and slowly rose to his feet. "Are ye Jacob's mob then?" he asked eyeing them warily. "If ye are then I want to join ye."

"Who are yer?" asked Riley not lowering his weapon. He cast his eyes around nervously, as if he expected a trap and to be attacked at any minute.

"Tom. Tom Moss – I'm a servant of Spark's," he said slowly lowering his hands. "I swear I'm alone, ain't no one else with me."

"And why would yer want ter join us?" asked Paddy gesturing at him with his loaded musket.

The young man raised his hands again and licked his lips nervously. "Same reason ye run off I s'pose. I've had enough of workin' for nothin' an' bein' flogged."

Aaron nodded in agreement with the young man. He thought the more men that joined them the better. They'd really be able to wreak havoc on the settlers if there were enough of them.

"Do any of the other lads from over there want ter join us?" asked Riley lowering his musket.

"Oh aye, but they're scared. They'll help ye if they can even if they don't join ye as such."

"Well welcome then," said Lawrie slapping him on the back. "So what are they calling us? Did yer say Jacob's mob?"

"Aye. Some are callin' ye that, an' some are callin' ye Jacob's Irish Brigade."

"Oh I like that," said Paddy shouldering his weapon.

"We're on our way ter raid Hicks' joint," said Riley handing him a pistol. "You're welcome ter come with us."

"Aye thank ye."

It was getting dark by the time the men reached William Hicks property. The faint glow of lamplight was emanating from the house, and Aaron thought he saw a light flickering in the barn as well. That could cause a problem. They didn't want to be caught unawares by someone returning to the house.

"I reckon someone's in the barn," he whispered to Riley.

Riley nodded and gestured to Lawrie to check it out. They waited while he quietly approached the barn and peered in the window. A moment later he returned.

"Aye Aaron's right. I reckon it's the good Lieutenant himself, making sure everything's in order for the night."

"Is he alone?" asked Riley. "Or was there someone with him?"

"No, no he's alone by the looks of it."

"Good. We'll be the ones surprisin' him in that case," said Riley with a grin. "Come on."

The five men quietly approached the house and stepped onto the front veranda. They could hear voices coming from inside. Aaron thought he heard a woman's voice among the other distinctly male conversation. They waited and listened for a moment. Riley held up four fingers which Aaron took to mean he thought there were four people in the house.

His heart was beating loudly in his ears and every muscle tensed as he waited for Riley to make a move. Time seemed to stop as he sucked in several deep breaths.

He held his musket across his arm ready to push his way into the house. Adrenalin was pulsing through him and he was breathing hard. A moment later Riley shoved the door open and they all piled into the house.

Mrs Hicks let out a scream of surprise and fright, while the two men who had been lounging at the kitchen table scrambled to their feet. It was too late. Riley and Paddy had their muskets aimed straight at them and they immediately surrendered.

"Shut up," snarled Lawrie pointing his pistol at Mrs Hicks who was about to let out another scream.

Aaron thought that would only increase her hysterics and was more than a little surprised when she abruptly shut her mouth. Her eyes were bugging out of her head as she stared at Lawrie, but at least she'd stopped yelling. They quickly secured the two men with ropes and shoved them into the corner on the floor. Paddy and Tom stood guard menacing them with their pistols.

"If they make a sound shoot them," said Riley breathing heavily. He took up a position by the front door and peered out.

There wasn't any sign of Hicks returning from the barn yet. He let out a breath and grinned around at the men. "Grab anythin' of value lads. An' Mrs Hick's, if you'd be so kind as ter prepare us some supper."

She stared open-mouthed at him.

"Now if yer please."

It took her a moment to gather her wits as she stared terrified around the room. Much to Aaron's relief, she started fumbling around in the kitchen. His stomach growled at the thought of a home-cooked supper.

Lawrie lit a candle and headed into the bedroom to search and Aaron joined him. The light from the candle cast shadows on the walls, but Aaron easily made out a dresser. He searched through it and found a brooch, a tortoiseshell comb and a silver thimble. He pocketed them before turning his attention to a large chest which Lawrie was already rifling through. That's when he noticed the cradle with a sleeping baby in it. He paused to look at it, all the while hoping it wouldn't wake up and start crying.

"There's a baby," he whispered to Lawrie.

Lawrie looked up from the chest alarmed. "Well for God sake don't wake it up!"

"Let's get out of here," said Aaron. The last thing he wanted to deal with was a crying baby and a hysterical woman.

They took several shirts and two warm jackets and quietly crept from the room, closing the door behind them. Paddy was packing ammunition and provisions in a bag and he looked up at them as they entered.

"What's a matter?" he asked.

"There's a baby asleep in there," said Aaron clearly startled by the discovery.

"Don't you hurt my baby," said Mrs Hicks turning from the stove and glaring at them.

"We won't touch yer baby," said Riley from the door. "Just git on with our supper."

A moment later the sound of boots on the veranda made them pause. Hicks was back from the barn. Mrs Hicks looked at them over her shoulder, until Lawrie pointed his pistol at her again. His message was clear and she quickly turned her back and returned to preparing their supper. The smell of frying bacon, beans and eggs was really starting to make Aaron salivate.

The door opened and Lieutenant Hicks entered. Aaron saw the confusion flit momentarily across his face as he took in the scene. It was quickly replaced by shock and outrage, but it was too late. Riley shut the door behind him and shoved the muzzle of his musket into his shoulder blades.

"Evenin'. I'll just be takin' that," he drawled taking the musket from Hicks' limp hand. "And I'll be havin' yer pocket watch as well," he said indicating the fob chain attached to his waistcoat.

Hicks glared at him but readily complied before turning his eyes to his wife. She had her back to him. "Are you alright Sophia?" he said. "You better not have hurt her."

"Not at all," said Riley as Lawrie and Aaron tied Hicks hands behind his back and shoved him into a chair. "Your lovely wife has shown us nothin' but fine hospitality."

Aaron saw her back stiffen, but she went on cooking their supper without a word. With all the men secured they continued their search of the house for any items of value. They found a small tin of cash which they took along with some pewter plates. There were several bottles of wine in the larder which they placed on the table. Riley found sufficient glasses and poured wine for them all.

Aaron had downed the first glass before Mrs Hicks put supper on the table. It was the first time in years any of them had sat down to a home-cooked supper. Aaron shoved the food into his mouth as fast as he could. He was starving and he noticed the others were doing the same. No one was talking and all he could hear was chewing and slurping. He smiled to himself.

They lounged around the table, satisfied and relaxed after such a hearty supper. Or perhaps it was the second glass of wine thought Aaron. It was making him feel a little giddy and light-headed, but he didn't care. He hadn't felt so content in a long while. He soaked up the last of his egg with a chunk of bread and held out his glass for another slug of wine.

Lieutenant Hicks glared at them from the end of the table but didn't say a word. Aaron noticed Mrs Hicks had quietly retreated into the other room and he wondered if Riley and the others would let her alone. He hadn't been in the company of a woman for so long that he would've liked her to stay. He glanced at Hick's and gulped down more of the wine. Perhaps if her husband was out of the way they could enjoy her company. He shook himself. What was he thinking? The woman had a young baby.

He had a mother and a sister and would not have them molested, and yet here he was imagining doing just that to the woman in the other room. He sucked in a deep breath and slowly let it out. What about Nellie? Oh God, he groaned. He remembered the last time he'd seen her when he was still a free man.

He'd been leaning against the dray as he waited for her to come out of the draper's store. He couldn't wait to see her, and every time the door opened his stomach did a somersault. He'd never felt that way about anyone before. Just thinking about her gave him an odd feeling in the pit of his stomach.

At twenty-three years of age, it was time he settled down, and he intended to - with Nellie. As soon as he had enough money to rent them a cottage he was going to speak to her father. That thought sent another odd feeling through him. He wasn't looking forward to speaking to Samuel Skinner about taking his daughter to wife. No, he didn't think he'd look kindly upon his offer. Not that he couldn't provide for Nellie; he could. He had a steady job working as a stonemason for old John Brewer. No, it wasn't that; he was steady and reliable.

He had acquired a reputation for sometimes being on the wrong side of the law. Last year he and James Barton had been accused of stealing liquor from the cellar of The Talbot Inn. The charges were eventually dropped because of lack of evidence against them. Still, some mud had stuck. He knew they'd been lucky to escape that one without some time in gaol.

Finally, the door to the drapers opened and Nellie stepped out. Her honey-

Jacob's Mob

blonde hair was scooped up and tied with loose ribbons. She spied Aaron immediately and gave him a gay wave as she made her way across the street. It gave him a chance to appreciate her slim figure as she stepped lightly over puddles and around several piles of manure.

"I hope you've not been waiting too long," she said tucking her hand into the crook of his arm. "Mrs Walker had a hundred and one chores for me to do today. I never thought I'd get away," she said smiling up at him.

"I don't mind waiting," he said as they strolled down the street towards the nearest tavern. "I've something to show you."

Nellie looked up at him with an inquisitive expression. "What?"

"Ah, you'll have to wait till we get to the George and Dragon. Then I'll show you."

"Oh I'm so curious to know what it is," she said hurrying her footsteps. "Is it a gift for me?"

Aaron grinned at her. He was delighted that she was so anxious to know what it was. "Well, aye I guess it could be a gift for you."

"Come on," she said dragging him into the tavern.

The warmth hit them as soon as they entered the dim interior. Aaron kept his arm firmly around Nellie's waist as he guided her away from the public bar and into the snug. He got them both a cider and joined her.

"Well?" she said impatiently.

He took off his jacket and rolled up his sleeve in order to show her his freshly tattooed arm. It was a love heart with two arrows piercing it. The initials AP and NS completed the love token. He waited, holding his breath while she peered at it.

"Oh Aaron," she sighed and looked into his eyes. "You can never forget me now."

"I never want to forget you," he said earnestly. "As soon as I've enough money I'll speak with your father."

"Oh make it soon. I so want to be your wife."

"I promise it'll be soon."

They finished their drinks and Aaron walked her home. She stopped with her hand on the gate and waited with her face tilted up to his. He kissed her softly before glancing up the street and towards the house - there was no one around. He took her in his arms and they kissed more passionately. Nellie leaned into him and he groaned as he felt her firm young breasts pushing into his chest. He reluctantly let her go. They were standing in the street he reminded himself. It would do his cause no good if they were seen.

"Will I see you tomorrow?" asked a breathless Nellie.

"Aye. I'll wait for you across the street." He watched her walk up the path to the door; her hips swaying seductively. He took several deep breaths. Their kiss had been more passionate than he'd intended, and he needed a few moments to compose himself. He grinned stupidly as he finally set off down the street for home.

He sighed as he took another mouthful of wine and pushed all thoughts of Nellie from his mind. He'd never see or hold her again. And nor would he molest an innocent woman who'd been so kind to cook his supper. He hoped the others wouldn't either.

It was nearing midnight before they departed Hicks' cabin. They were all well inebriated and loaded with provisions and firearms. They also had a few items of value that they planned to trade for information. All in all, it had been a successful raid and Aaron barely felt the cold as he huddled under his blanket at the back of the shallow cave.

~

Chapter Five

Wallis Plains, August 1825

News of the bushranger's raid on
Lieutenant Hicks' caused outrage among the
settlers. They demanded immediate action
be taken. Captain Allman arrived with three
soldiers from Newcastle with instructions to
pursue and capture them. They were joined
by local Magistrate Alexander Scott. The
search party assembled at Don McLeod's
property and waited for the native trackers
to arrive. George McIntire had been sent to
fetch the two natives who'd assisted in the
initial search for the runaways back in July.

Don McLeod leaned against the
railing on the veranda surveying his yard.
The August storms had arrived early
bringing torrential rain and strong winds.
His yard was awash and knee-deep in mud
which the horses had churned into a
quagmire. He wondered if Scott had any
hope of tracking the bushrangers in this
weather even with Mullabuy and

Bandagrun's help. Inwardly he didn't think they any chance of finding them, but he kept his thoughts to himself.

Alexander Scott was well known for being somewhat of a zealot and Don knew he'd only antagonise him by suggesting they wait for the weather to clear.

"Any idea how long your man's going to be fetching the natives?" asked Alexander Scott joining him on the veranda. "We really need to get underway before we lose the light."

"I'm sure he'll be along soon," replied Don politely. "We don't always know where the natives are or if they'll be coerced into tracking for us. We'll just have to wait and see."

"Hrmph," said Scott clearly impatient at the delay. "Captain Allman perhaps we can go it alone?"

Captain Allman had just joined the other two on the veranda. He shook himself and stamped the mud off his boots. Don looked him up and down and wished he'd removed the mud before stepping onto the veranda. His wife would be most unhappy if it was walked into the house. Henry Allman was an unremarkable-looking man. He would be hard to describe with his ordinary brown hair and narrow blue eyes. His manner was also plain and to the point.

"No," he replied.

Don hid a wry smile, while Alexander Scott let out another sound of obvious annoyance. There was nothing that could be done to hurry McIntire back with the trackers, and there was no point heading off without them.

Much to Alexander's relief he didn't have to wait too long. McIntire arrived back with the two trackers, not more than twenty minutes later. It was still raining steadily but he was impatient to be off. He wanted to be the one to capture the bushrangers and put an end to their rampage. He very much expected to not only secure them but for his neighbours to bestow their undying gratitude upon him. Not only that, but he would see to it that they were severely punished for their depredation; hanging would be too good for them.

"Next time I see you, Mr McLeod I'll have them croppies in custody," he said stepping off the veranda. "Mark my words."

"I wish you luck Mr Scott, and I hope you're right."

He mounted his horse and the small search party headed off. Mullabuy took the lead heading northeast from McLeod's. They followed the river past James Reid's place where it had broken its bank causing floodwater to spread out over the low lying plain. They were forced to head for higher ground, keeping well clear of the flooded river until they came to Lieutenant Hicks property.

Mullabuy and Bandagrun spent the next twenty minutes deciphering the various tracks leading in and out from the house and yard until they finally agreed the bushrangers had gone northeast.

They mounted up again and followed the two trackers north back through Reid's property. Alexander Scott was confident they'd be successful as they followed the trail up into the low lying hills. It was still raining steadily as they traversed up and down the undulating hills. They waded through several swollen creeks as they continued to move ever northward.

It was as they were following one of these flooded creeks that the two trackers came to a halt. They stopped at a part of the creek where the bank had collapsed causing a mudslide. To Scott's eye, it was nothing but a pile of mud that had slid down the embankment, but the two natives had apparently seen something else.

"Dey was camped here," said Mullabuy spreading his arms out towards the mud. "But dey gone now."

Bandagrun nodded in agreement and then began searching the area. Alexander presumed he was looking for clues as to which way the bushrangers had gone. He sat back in his saddle and waited. The cold wind sent a shiver through him as it blew its icy fingers under the collar of his coat. The area was heavily treed with gums and acacias which were providing some shelter from the rain, but the wind was whipping through the undergrowth.

"Which way?" said Alexander impatiently. He wanted to get on with it and catch up to them before nightfall.

The two natives carefully searched the area for at least fifteen minutes, but they didn't appear to have picked up the trail. Alexander was getting more impatient by the moment. He shifted uneasily in his saddle as he scanned the bush for any signs. He couldn't see anything that suggested which way they might've gone, and he groaned with frustration. Their tracks had obviously been obliterated by the rain and the trackers had no idea. He wanted to yell at them, but sat quietly, breathing heavily.

After what seemed like hours the two trackers finally agreed on a direction. Mullabuy pointed south indicating that the men had crossed the swollen creek. Alexander surveyed the flooded creek dubiously. What was usually a gurgling brook was now a swift torrent rushing headlong over the rocks and creating swirling eddies.

The bushrangers must've crossed before it became so flooded. He gave Captain Allman and the soldiers a nod and plunged his horse into the frigid waters.

~

Aaron shivered, not just from the abysmal cold but from the close shave they'd just had. It had been raining almost non-stop for days but they'd been relatively dry in their muddy cave until this morning.

"It looks like our cave's sprung a leak," said Lawrie shuffling himself towards the opening. "Shit, my breeches are soaked."

Sure enough, water was seeping into the back of the cave causing small rivulets to wend their way through the mud. Aaron thought they looked like small rivers, branching out as they made their way to the ocean.

"Our supplies are getting wet as well," said Tom scrambling into the back of the cave.

He grabbed a sack of flour and hauled it away from what was starting to become a deluge. Aaron took it from him and tossed it clear. Tom handed him a pouch of tobacco before diving back into the back of the cave. He hauled out the small box of valuables before crawling back in to get the rest of their supplies.

"Grab whatever you can," said Aaron taking the box and handing it to Lawrie who was now at the cave entrance. He was gathering their firearms together which were wrapped blankets to keep them dry.

Tom had his head and shoulders right in the back of the cave when the whole lot gave way. The roof and back wall collapsed half burying Tom and engulfing the cave in slippery mud. Riley and Paddy were sitting near the cave opening and jumped clear as the mud slid its way to the opening.

"Shit," said Lawrie dropping the firearms and blankets. He stared wide-eyed at Tom's legs which were the only part of him now visible.

"Fuck," yelled Aaron scrambling to get clear of the mud. "Grab Tom!"

Lawrie and Aaron each grabbed hold of one of Tom's legs and pulled as hard as they could. Aaron could feel the adrenaline coursing through his blood as they hauled him clear of the mudslide. He emerged coughing and spluttering and covered in mud. Aaron sucked in several deep breaths and stared at him.

"Shit are yer awright?" said Paddy helping him to his feet.

He was badly shaken but alive. "Aye I think so," he said as he trying to wipe the mud from his face.

"Shit yer covered in mud," said Lawrie handing him a relatively dry blanket.

"Thanks," he said using a corner of it to wipe his face before wrapping it around himself. "I thought I was done for."

"Aye so did we," said Riley surveying Tom and what was left of their camp.

It was now a pile of mud. Most of their provisions had been lost but they still had their firearms and a small supply of dry firewood. Tom had managed to grab the small box of valuables so all was not lost. The creek was rising rapidly and Aaron thought they'd need to cross it soon if they hoped to head south.

"We should get going while we can still cross the creek," he said.

"Aye. We'll need ter find a new campsite," replied Riley eyeing the creek. "We should head south."

They gathered up the few provisions that had been saved and headed south across the flooded creek. They'd need to find a new place to camp before nightfall. They turned east away from the rising floodwaters of the river and continued for another half an hour.

"I'm sure there's a farmhouse not fer from here," said Paddy coming to a halt. "It belongs ter McClymont an' he's bound to have fresh provisions. I've been there once before."

"Aye. Which way do yer reckon?" said Riley stopping and looking at Paddy.

He glanced around for a minute or two trying to get his bearings. "I reckon it's up this way," he said pointing towards to east. "It won't be fer."

They trudged on for another mile or so before they spied a farmhouse nestled amongst some gum trees. It was a typical looking timber cabin and it looked deserted. They crouched under the cover of several

Lilly pilly bushes while they surveyed the scene.

"I'm pretty sure no one's home," said Paddy gesturing with his hands. "There ain't no smoke coming outta there, an' I reckon this is McClymont's farm. He ain't up here too often."

"I reckon you're right," said Lawrie standing up and stretching. "Come on."

They approached the house and stepped onto the back porch. The door was locked and the place certainly looked deserted. There were no sounds coming from inside and Riley peered in the window.

"Ain't no one in there," he said shoving his shoulder against the door and giving it a firm push.

It took several more shoves from Riley and Paddy, but eventually, the door gave way and they piled inside. It didn't smell damp or musty like no one had inhabited the place for a while. Aaron expected McClymont could return at any time. Two doors were leading off from the small kitchen, and the men quickly spread out to search the place.

Tom and Aaron went through into a bedroom. It was obviously the main bedroom as a double bed took up most of it. Aaron stripped off the warm looking quilt that was on it, while Tom opened the large chest under the window and began pulling clothes out of it. He stripped off his wet muddy clothes and put on clean dry ones. They were a bit big for him, but Aaron doubted he cared. He must have been freezing in the mud sodden ones he'd been wearing.

They went back into the kitchen, where Paddy already had a bag of flour, rice and dried peas stacked on the small wooden table. Riley emerged from the other room with a musket and two dry blankets under his arm.

"I reckon we ought ter stay 'ere the night," said Lawrie grinning at them. "It's warm an' dry an' ain't no one home."

"Aye good idea," said Paddy dumping a cask of salt pork on the table. "I'll get the fire going fer supper."

Aaron had a nervous feeling about being at McClymont's. He peered outside half expecting to see someone coming, but the yard was deserted. The others seemed unperturbed. Paddy was already getting the fire going, and Lawrie was laying out their wet blankets to dry.

"I was thinkin' we ought ter trade some of them baubles we stole from Hicks," said Riley sitting down on one of the four chairs. "We nearly bloody lost them today."

"Aye," replied Aaron. "It would be good to know who's out looking for us, and how many there are."

"Who'd tell us?" asked Lawrie sitting down and putting his head in his hands.

"I reckon Tom Boardman would help us fer sure," said Paddy turning from the woodstove. He had a small fire going which was starting to radiate some heat into the small kitchen.

"Aye yer right," said Riley his face lighting up. "He used ter be a croppy just like us, an' I reckon his wife would like some of them trifles."

"Do yer reckon he'd know what's going on?" said Lawrie.

"Oh aye he'd know," said Paddy confidently. "He lives near town an' he's a horse doctor. I bet he knows everything that's going on."

Lawrie nodded in agreement.

"Well it's decided then," said Riley grinning. "We'll go pay Tom a visit in the mornin'."

The following morning it was raining steadily and the men were in no hurry to leave the warm dry cabin. Aaron was anxious. He wanted to leave as soon as possible. He'd spent a restless night half expecting someone to burst in on them. He had to concede that it had been a relief to get out of the rain and cold, but now he wanted to go. He looked nervously out of the window at the rain-soaked yard. He sighed. It was going to be another cold and uncomfortable day, and he had no idea where they'd find shelter for the night.

Paddy baked a batch of Johnny cakes that would suffice for their midday meal on the way to Boardman's house. They wrapped their firearms and provisions in blankets in an effort to keep them as dry as possible. Finally, much to Aaron's relief, they left McClymont's just before midday, by which time the rain had eased to an annoying drizzle.

They headed west from McClymont's back towards the river. Tom Boardman's house was on the outskirts of Wallis Plains on the south side of the bridge. It would take them a couple of hours to get there as long as they had no mishaps on the way. They kept as close to the river as the floodwaters allowed. It was easier going with less undergrowth, and in several places, they were able to follow a wallaby trail.

It was mid-afternoon when they crossed to the south side of the river and made their way along a worn dirt track. Tom's house was situated high on the riverbank, and the men approached it with caution. The back yard went all the way down to the steep embankment and contained several outbuildings. These included a large barn as well as an open-fronted shed which was being used as a stable. They paused behind the barn and surveyed the yard. Aaron breathed deeply as they waited to see if Tom had any customers in the yard. After five or so minutes of waiting Riley let out a deep breath.

"Awright, I reckon it's clear," he said. "Let's go."

He stepped out from behind the barn with the others right behind him. They crossed the yard to the back door where Riley paused and glanced around for a final time. Aaron also scanned the yard nervously. It was empty and there were no sounds or voices of anyone coming. Riley knocked firmly on the door.

It was opened a moment later by a middle-aged woman with her greying hair pulled back into a tight bun. She peered at them for a moment.

"Tom," she said turning her head and calling to someone in the house.

Riley smiled at the woman and waited. Aaron held his breath. He knew of Tom Boardman, but he'd never actually met him. He hoped Paddy and Riley knew him or this could end with him calling the local constable, and them having to run.

A few moments later a large mousy haired man came to the door. He looked at them warily. Aaron didn't see any sign on his broad face that he recognised them.

"Afternoon. Do yer remember me? Patrick Riley?"

"Aye I thought it might be ye," he said still eyeing them warily. "So ye've done a runner?"

"Aye we have," said Riley unperturbed. "We have some things we thought might interest yer an' yer wife if yer willin' ter help us that is."

Tom Boardman stood in the doorway glancing from one to the other for at least a minute. Aaron thought he saw some speculation in his brown eyes.

"Aye," he said at last as he stepped back to let them in.

Aaron let out the breath he'd been holding as he followed Riley into the house. They stepped straight into a small kitchen which had a large wooden table in the middle of it. It took up most of the available room. Tom closed the door before turning his attention back to Riley.

"So what do ye want to know?" he said matter of factly. "I'm presumin' ye want information?"

"Aye," said Riley grinning and turning to Lawrie. "Give me the box so we can show Tom here what we've got."

Lawrie nodded and reached into the inside pocket of his jacket and brought a small wooden box. He handed it to Riley who opened it and peered inside.

"I think Mrs Boardman will like this," he said pulling a sapphire brooch from the box.

He smiled at Mrs Boardman, who up until this time had been standing back behind her husband. She stepped forward to take a better look and reached her hand out for the brooch. Riley dropped it into the palm of her hand and snapped the box shut.

"Tis a lovely thing," said Riley grinning.

"Aye," she said looking at her husband. "I like it very much."

Tom Boardman grunted but Aaron noticed his eyes softened as he gazed at his wife. She was obviously delighted with the brooch and he suspected Tom Boardman liked to please her.

"As I said. What do ye want to know?" said Tom Boardman turning his attention back to Riley.

"Well, firstly do yer know who's out searchin' for us, an' if they've got trackers?"

"Aye. Alexander Scott. He's the Magistrate around here," he said nodding. "He's got soldiers come up from Newcastle with him, an' he's got a couple of native trackers as well."

"Shit," said Paddy. "They must really want ter get us."

"Aye. I reckon they do," said Tom. "Ye've caused an uproar in these parts."

"Well thank yer," said Riley. "I wonder if we could ask one more thing of yer?"

"Aye," said Tom warily.

"Do yer mind if we stay the night in yer barn?"

Tom glanced over his shoulder at his wife. She looked at them all with her bright blue eyes before giving the briefest nod.

"Aye, but ye'll be gone at daybreak," said Tom turning back to Riley.

"Aye. Thank yer," said Riley smiling. "Come on lads." He gestured to Aaron to open the door of the Boardman's small kitchen. "Afternoon ma'am," he said to Mrs Boardman before walking out the door.

The men settled themselves in the barn for the night. It was relatively warm and dry amongst the bales of hay although they were only able to have a meagre supper. There was nowhere they could light a fire to cook, so their supper consisted of a few Johnny cakes and hard biscuits. Aaron didn't mind the simple supper. He was glad to be out of the cold and rain for another night. He hoped the rain would ease off tomorrow, although he didn't hold out much of hope of that actually happening.

~

Chapter Six

Wallis Plains

They left the comfort of the Boardman's barn at first light. It was a freezing morning with a hard frost covering the ground. Aaron wrapped his blanket around his shoulders as they headed down the embankment towards the river. At least it was dry for the moment, although the sky looked dark and ominous. Aaron sighed as they walked along the river bank. He hoped they'd find a dry sheltered campsite where they could huddle down for a couple of days.

"I know of a nice dry hut down on Spark's property," said Tom as they trudged through the bush. He sounded grumpy and discontent to Aaron's ears, and he didn't blame him. He could barely feel his frozen toes.

Riley raised a quizzical brow at him. "Sounds good if yer want ter git caught."

"No, no. Tis deserted, ain't no one ever go there," he replied.

Aaron paused and surveyed the dark overcast sky. He was freezing and they'd be soaked before long by the look of the clouds; the thought of a nice dry hut sounded almost too good to be true.

"Perhaps we should check it out?"

"Aye we should," said Tom, encouraged by Aaron's words. "I swear no one will even know we're there. No one goes down that way."

"I'm all for it," said Lawrie shivering.

"Even getting caught?" said Paddy shifting his load. "I ain't going back ter that damn Jacob's."

Riley stopped and looked at them all. Aaron glanced around as well. They all looked cold and miserable. After spending the last two nights under cover the thought of camping out in wet clothes huddled around a smoky fire was not very appealing. He hoped they'd find somewhere dry to make camp, but he doubted that anywhere dry existed.

"Alright," said Riley at last. "Lead the way, Tom."

"Aye," he said smiling happily as he took the lead.

Tom led them eastward passed the bridge and down the other side towards the Wallis Creek. They hadn't followed the creek very far when the skies opened and it began to pour. They hurried along as fast as they could hoping to find somewhere to shelter until the rain stopped. Lawrie came to a stop and pointed to what looked like little more than a rocky ledge. They had to squat down to get in under it and there was barely enough room for all of them, but it was better than nothing. The five of them squeezed in and sat there huddled out of the rain.

They remained there for most of the day. When the rain finally stopped they crawled out from under the ledge. They set off for the hut again but didn't get far before it started to pour again. It began to get heavier as they trudged on through the bush. They had everything wrapped in blankets including their firearms to try and keep them dry. Aaron hoped they'd find somewhere dry to camp soon but didn't hold out much hope. After going on for another half mile Riley came to a halt.

"I reckon we ought ter camp here for the night," he said dropping his load.

No one argued. It was getting late in the day and Aaron didn't think they'd make it to the hut on Spark's property before dark.

They were close to the river where there were a number of large callistemon bushes and tall river gums. They cut several saplings and made a rough shelter which they covered in branches. They stashed their box of valuables at the back of the shelter under some leaf mould and branches. Aaron shoved their wrapped firearms to the back as well to keep them as dry as possible.

In no time, Tom and Lawrie had a small smoky fire going and had the billy on to make tea. Paddy busied himself preparing supper. Aaron huddled under the shelter by the fire trying to get some warmth into his bones. He hoped this would be the last night they'd spend out in the bush. The hut Tom had mentioned sounded like a Godsend.

~

Alexander Scott's search party had been out scouring the bush for the outlaws for five days. He was wet and chilled to the bone; tired and totally frustrated at their progress. He had to concede that Mullabuy and Bandagrun had done a good job so far, but they'd lost the trail and none of them had any idea which way to go. The rain had gotten heavier in the last hour or so and Alexander knew they'd have to stop and make camp soon.

They were down by the river following it an easterly direction. It was slow going with the horses as this part of the riverbank was covered in large Callistemon bushes. They were pushing their way through them when the native trackers came to an abrupt halt and crouched down behind one of the large shrubs. Alexander dismounted and tossed his reins to one of the soldiers.

"What is it?" he said joining the two trackers.

"Smoke," said Mullabuy pointing through the trees.

At first, Alexander couldn't see a thing. The pouring rain was obscuring everything from view, but as he strained to see he finally saw it – a wisp of blue smoke curling up through the tree trunks. It had to be them. His heart started thumping with excitement at the thought of having the buggers in custody. He crept back away from the bushes to where Captain Allman was waiting with the soldiers.

"It's them, I'm sure of it," he said excitedly. "They've got a fire going. I suggest we go on foot from here if we have any chance of surprising them."

"Aye," said Captain Allman dismounting.

They hobbled the horses and began walking as quietly as possible towards the smoke. As they neared Alexander could hear several voices and was just able to make out a lean-to shelter. He stopped and gestured to Allman and the soldiers to surround them. His heart was hammering in his ears, but he was sure they hadn't heard them approaching. As soon as the men were in position he rushed the shelter.

It was all over in a moment. The five men looked up in surprise as Alexander yelled out. Their weapons were out of reach and faced with five muskets pointing at them the bushrangers surrendered without a fight.

Alexander wasted no time in securing them with handcuffs and then tied them one to the other. He had no intention of giving them any opportunity to escape custody on the way back to McLeod's farm. He was delighted that they'd captured them so easily. They'd caught them completely unawares in the midst of cooking their supper. Their weapons were wrapped in blankets and quite useless to them.

Alexander's blood was thrumming with the excitement of capturing them that he hardly noticed the rain. He became almost impervious to the cold and wet as they made their way back to McLeod's. It was well past dark by the time they entered his yard and lodged their prisoners in his barn under guard. They would have to wait until morning to hand them over at the Barracks in Wallis Plains.

~

Aaron shifted uncomfortably. His hands were handcuffed and he was tied so close to Lawrie that he could barely move. He was chilled to the bone and he shivered. The manacles were digging into his flesh and try as he might he couldn't find a comfortable position.

The last time he'd been chained was when he'd arrived in Portsmouth before they put him on the hulk. After hours travelling from Oxford in the stuffy compartment, he sucked in a lungful of fresh air as soon as the door was opened. It smelled of the sea, rotting timber and shit.

"Out," said the guard gesturing to the man closest to the open door.

Aaron waited until it was his turn before climbing down out of the cart and stretching. He'd had very little room to move with nearly twenty men crammed in together and his legs had become stiff and cramped. The guard gave him a prod in the direction of an open doorway and he quickly followed the other men inside. He had to duck his head as he entered the low slung building.

The walls were lined with large wooden troughs and there were several chairs in the middle. A long bench at the end was piled high with uniforms. Aaron immediately realised they would be washing and putting on clean clothes. He hadn't had a change of clothes in weeks and relished the thought of feeling clean. He didn't wait to be told; he immediately set to undressing.

"Remove all your clothes," one of the guards was saying as he walked up and down. "There's soap for ye to use."

James joined him at the trough and smirked at him. "You know you stink don't you?"

"Aye," said Aaron lathering the soap. "And what, do you think you smell any better?"

James grinned at him as he grabbed the soap and proceeded to lather it as well. "No, I don't reckon I do."

One of the guards came along with a hard rubbing brush and proceeded to scrub Aaron down. It was like a stiff birch broom on his skin and he recoiled. It was so rough he thought it'd take his skin off rather than clean it.

"Stand still."

He gritted his teeth and endured it - all the time glaring at the man who wasn't satisfied until his skin was chaffed red raw and bleeding in places. Just when Aaron thought he couldn't take another moment of it he stopped and turned his attentions to James. Aaron pressed his lips together and breathed heavily through his nose. He dared not say a word.

"Sit," another guard said to him.

He turned around and saw that some of the other men were already seated and having their hair cut. He didn't think that could be any worse than being scrubbed down. He sat down and waited while his hair was clipped as close to his skull as the scissors would allow. He was then handed a set of clean slops. He dressed in the shirt, breeches and yellow waistcoat. They were too big for him, except for the trousers which were a bit short. A blue woollen jacket and cap completed his prisoner's outfit. He really didn't care. It felt so good to be clean, even if had been roughly done.

Once all the men were dressed the guard opened the door and marched them across a small courtyard to the blacksmiths. Aaron's heart was hammering in his chest as fear gripped him. He felt like he was suffocating as he entered the smithy's shop. There was only one reason that he could think of why they would need a blacksmith - leg irons. He swallowed and glanced sideways at James who looked as pale and sweaty as he felt. He could see the apprehension in his eyes as they waited. God help them.

The smithy worked efficiently as he riveted weighted ankle rings to each man. These were connected by eight links to a ring in the centre. A strap was then fastened to the centre ring and then to the waistband of his breeches. Aaron had no idea how he was going to get used to carrying around fifteen pounds of iron on each leg.

"You look like a trussed-up pig," whispered James. "All ready for Christmas."

"Shut it," said the nearest guard giving James a shove.

Aaron groaned inwardly. One of these days James' humour would get them both into real trouble. As soon as all the men had been fitted with their chains they were herded outside and marched down to the dock. The irons gave Aaron such an odd feeling as he walked down to the waiting longboat. His normal gait wasn't possible and he found he had to take shorter steps to accommodate the centre ring.

He managed to step into the longboat without falling headlong and sat down. A few minutes later they pushed off from the docks and the oarsmen began rowing. It was late in the day and a cool breeze was blowing off the water. Aaron shivered. It wasn't just the cold air that made him shudder, however. Ahead he could see the rotting hulk that they were being rowed towards. He'd heard about the hulks – everyone had. The old warships that were no longer seaworthy had been refitted to house prisoners waiting for transportation. He just never imagined he'd see one up close.

The oars were raised as the longboat bumped against the hull of the hulk. Aaron could see a timber ramp-like structure protruding from the side of the ship. Several soldiers who were standing on it grabbed the ropes that were tossed to them securing the smaller craft. Aaron and James were sitting about halfway down the boat, so they waited while the prisoners at the front disembarked.

Aaron's insides were squirming – partly nerves and partly fear. Actually more from fear, he admitted to himself. He'd heard stories about the treatment of prisoners on the hulks, and he swallowed the lump that had formed in the back of his throat. He felt parched and pressed his lips together as he surveyed the scene.

A minute later he was roughly hauled to his feet and prodded to board the hulk. He swayed as he lost his balance. He tried to brace himself but he was unused to the weight of the heavy irons. He was waving his arms about trying to regain his balance when one of the guards grabbed him and shoved him forward. He would've landed flat in the bottom of the boat if he hadn't been so close to the man in front. He slammed into the man's back and seized hold of his shoulders finally righting himself.

"Sorry," he mumbled.

"Quiet," shouted the guard behind him giving him another prod in his shoulder blades.

Aaron shuffled to the front of the boat and lifting one leg at a time climbed off onto the ramp. He quickly looked around for James. Oh good, he was right behind him. He was fearful of losing sight of him – having James with him gave him the courage to deal with whatever lay ahead. Without him, he wasn't so sure. He stepped aside and urged James to go ahead of him. Their eyes met for a brief moment, each reflecting the fear they were both feeling.

The waiting soldiers urged him forward towards a narrow ladder. He noticed the men ahead of him were putting both feet on the rung before trying to go up another step. He did the same and managed to navigate his way up to the top without falling. He took a deep breath and quickly took in his surroundings before another soldier gave him a shove.

"Keep going."

He had to bow his head slightly or else he'd have hit it on the ceiling. He was standing on the lowest deck which had been fitted out as a mess. Rows of roughly hewn tables and benches lined the walls leaving a narrow walkway down the middle.

A clerk was sitting at one of the tables with a large ledger open before him, his quill scratching the parchment. Aaron shifted his weight and waited while he asked each man his name. When it was his turn he gave his name and waited while the clerk found it on the page.

"Four oh forty seven."

His eyes didn't leave the page and Aaron was left with the uncomfortable feeling that he no longer mattered. He'd been reduced to a number and his stomach did an uncomfortable somersault at the thought. Was this to be his life now? He'd been sentenced to transportation for life – did that mean he wasn't Aaron Price anymore? Anger threatened to overtake him and he sucked in several large breaths and tried to remain calm. He had no intention of giving them any reason to flog him or worse.

"Keep moving."

He barely noticed as he climbed the ladder to the next deck. He wondered if

James was feeling the same, or in his normal style had he just shrugged it off. He thought the latter. James was like that. He didn't think he could ever be like that. Anger always overtook him before he could think clearly. Just like his Pa. That thought sat uncomfortably and he tried to push it aside as he followed James up to the next deck. He wasn't like his father; wouldn't be like his father.

This deck was divided into compartments with a corridor down the middle, and he could see several guards directing the new arrivals. The ceiling wasn't quite as low as it had been on the lower decks, but Aaron still had to bend his head slightly.

"Ward twenty-four," said the guard indicating to one of the prisoners a few ahead of James.

He waved his hand indicating they should follow and counted off the next twelve prisoners including James and Aaron. The compartment was small and empty. Aaron glanced around then shrugged at James, who looked just as perplexed. The other inmates of their compartment clearly didn't know what was going on either.

"You'll find the hammocks stowed in the bulkhead," said a guard stopping in the doorway. "Three eight twenty three will show you. Half an hour to supper."

Supper? Paddy had been in the midst of preparing their supper when the damned soldiers had surprised them. Aaron doubted they'd be getting anything to eat tonight. His stomach grumbled and his arms ached but there was no relief. At least the barn was dry, that was something.

~

Chapter Seven

They were woken at daybreak and each given a bowl of thin porridge. They were all ravenous and Aaron ate hungrily tipping the bowl greedily into his mouth. They were then hauled to their feet and loaded onto the back of a cart. The rain had stopped but there was a freezing cold wind blowing and the frost was thick on the ground.

Aaron shivered as the cart slowly headed off. They were under the guard of Captain Allman and the soldiers from Newcastle. Aaron briefly wondered what awaited them. He expected they'd send them to Sydney for trial, and then what? A flogging and gaol or would they hang them? He swallowed and pressed his lips together as he remembered the last time he'd been tried for burglary.

He and James had been the last of the prisoners to be tried that day. The guard had led them down a short corridor from the waiting cell to the Courtroom. At the end was a large heavy oak door which was opened by two guards as they approached. This was it. Aaron was breathing heavily as he followed James into the Courtroom.

The oak-panelled walls made the Court appear small and overcrowded. The Jury of twelve men seated along one wall in three rows. The bewigged Judge was already seated at a long bench opposite where he and James were standing. Aaron thought he looked rather tired and unhappy. That may not bode well.

The Clerk rose to his feet and read the charges from a large parchment.

"James Barton and Aaron Price are indicted for burglariously breaking and entering the dwelling house of William Robinson, at about 1 o'clock in the morning on the 18th of February at Clanfield. They are charged with stealing twelve hats, two aprons and a pocket watch to the value of six pounds and two shillings."

He promptly sat down, folded the parchment and took up his quill. Aaron gazed around the room, wondering if George and Frances Barton had come – and Nellie. There were several people seated in a small gallery behind the main bench. He couldn't help the feeling of hope that washed over him at the thought that Nellie might have come. It lasted no more than a second - she wasn't there, but the Barton's were. He was glad for James, and himself. He really didn't want Nellie to bear witness to his fate. He sucked in his breath and waited.

A tall bespectacled man then stood up and addressed the Judge. "I call my first witness," he said in a loud clear voice. "Mr John Billings of Clanfield."

A rather stout man wearing a waistcoat that looked too small for him took to the witness stand. He was a large barrel-chested man with huge biceps. Aaron stared at him wide-eyed. No wonder he'd taken the wind out him, he was lucky he hadn't broken his back when he landed on him.

"Mr Billings, would you please tell the court what occurred on the night."

John Billings cleared his throat. "I live next door to the Robinson's house, which has a rear garden. I knew that they were away for a few days on a family matter." He paused and looked around the

Court like he was making an important point and he didn't want anyone to miss it. "Anyways, I heard a noise comin' from their back garden, an' soon after I heard more noises comin' from their house. I went out an' saw their garden gate was open."

"Did you see anyone?" asked the Prosecutor.

"Aye. A short time later I seen two men climbin' out of Robinson's window. I quickly shut the gate an' tied it with a length of rope, trappin' them in the garden. I then asked 'em what business they had there. "

"And what business did they have Mr Billings?"

"None that was any good," he said indignantly. "So I called for the Watch. He came an' between the two of us we apprehended the pair."

"Thank you, Mr Billings," said the Prosecutor indicating for him to leave the stand. "I call Mr Thomas Baker to give witness."

Thomas Baker was a tall sullen-looking man with stringy blonde hair. He glared sourly at Aaron and James as he made his way to the stand. Aaron glared back at him.

"Mr Baker would you please tell the court what occurred on the night?"

"Aye. I'm a Watchman of Clanfield. I was doing me usual rounds when I heard Mr Billings calling for me. I immediately hurried to assist 'im. He says to me he has two thieves bailed up in Robinson's garden. They put up a bit of a fight, but we secured 'em and took 'em to the Watch-House."

"Did they have any of the stolen goods mentioned?"

"Oh aye. They'd hidden a bag under a bush which was stuffed full of everything they stole."

"And finally Mr Baker. Were you able to ascertain how Mr Robinson's house was broken into?"

"Oh aye," he replied happily. "They'd taken a brace an' bit an' bored holes into his window shutter. From there twould 'ave been easy enough to jimmy open the window."

"Thank you, Mr Baker," he said before turning to the Judge. "Your Honor I rest the case for the King before the Jury."

"Thank you, Mr Barnard," said the Judge rousing himself. "Do the prisoner's offer any defence?"

James glanced sideways at Aaron and gave him a nod. The two had spent hours deciding what defence they might give if they had the opportunity. They'd decided Aaron would do the talking, but now that the time was here he felt like his mouth was full of sand. He licked his lips and cleared his throat. He took a couple of deep breaths in through his nose and glanced nervously around the Courtroom.

"Aye," he said, at last, taking a step forward and placing his hands on the oak railing. "We'd been drinking at the public house, and were on our way home when this man grabs us and shoves us into Robinson's garden. Before we knew what was happening, he'd shut the gate and locked us in. He then says we're robbers and starts calling for the Watch."

There were several murmurs from the Jurors, but otherwise, the Court was quiet. All except for the scratching noise of the Clerk's quill as he busily wrote down the proceedings.

"The Jury well know their job and will now consider the evidence before them and deliver their verdict," said the Judge speaking directly to the jurors.

The jurors rose and filed out of the Courtroom. Aaron presumed they were going off to some antechamber to discuss their decision. He wasn't confident that he and James had put any doubt in their minds. He knew the evidence against them was damning, but he couldn't help but hope they might have believed them. He glanced across at the gallery where George and Frances Barton were seated. If they had any thoughts at all they were keeping them well hidden. They were both sitting there like a pair of stone statues. He sighed and wondered how long they would have to wait.

It wasn't long. In less than fifteen minutes the Jurors filed back into the Courtroom and took up their seats. Aaron's heart was hammering in his chest as the anxiety he was feeling threatened to overwhelm him. He breathed deeply and hung onto the railing in front of him. He closed his eyes and said a heartfelt prayer.

"Have you the Jury reached a decision?" asked the Judge.

"Aye we have Your Honor," said a rather stout middle-aged man standing up. "We find the defendants guilty as charged."

Aaron thought he might be sick.

"Thank you. You have discharged your duty honourably," said the Judge before turning his attention to the two prisoners. "James Barton and Aaron Price. You have been found guilty of the indictment against you, and it is the decision of this Court that you be hanged from the neck until you are dead." He paused before gesturing to the guard. "Take them away."

Nothing had prepared Aaron for those words. He knew the penalty they were facing was death, but to actually hear that sentence handed down was another matter. His legs felt like they belonged to someone else. His whole body was shaking, and he gulped in air like he was drowning as he shuffled from the Court. God, how was he going to get through this? He didn't know. The hollow feeling of helplessness in the pit of his stomach began spreading outwards to the rest of his body like a crawling infestation. He was glad Nellie hadn't come; in the end, he was glad his mother wasn't there either.

The fear gripped him now as it had then. It squirmed around in his belly like a living thing curdling his breakfast. He gagged as sour bile rose in the back of his throat. Shit, he'd been stupid!

~

It was a cold, cramped, uncomfortable journey in the back of the cart. Aaron thought they'd only be taking them as far as Wallis Plains, but that was a few miles away. They'd probably have to wait for a boat to come up river to take them to Newcastle. He really didn't want to think about what might lie ahead. He glanced around at his companions. They all looked about as unhappy and uncomfortable as he was. He sighed.

He'd just about lost all feeling in his cramped legs by the time the cart came to a halt outside what he thought must be the Wallis Plains Barracks. It was an unremarkable weathered timber building with bars on the windows. He sucked in a deep breath as he climbed down from the cart.

They were led inside, still tied to one another and put in the one and only holding cell. It was small and cramped with the five of them in there, and there was already another man who appeared to be asleep on a narrow crib. Aaron briefly wondered what he'd done to

find himself here before he was roughly turned around and his manacles were removed. He rubbed his arms where the skin had been rubbed raw by the handcuffs. Their gaolers chained a padlock to the door and left. He could hear them down the hall talking and laughing.

"Shit," said Riley sitting down on the empty narrow crib. "I'm sorry lads. It looks like we've hit the end of the road."

"Aye," said Paddy looking around the dismally small cell. "Oh well, we all knew what we were in fer didn't we?"

Aaron noticed that while Tom was nodding in agreement and looking downcast at their prospects, Lawrie appeared to be inspecting their new accommodation. He was looking everywhere and running his hands over the timber walls.

"What is it?" asked Aaron raising his dark brows at him.

Lawrie ignored him and continued to explore the small cell. Not that there was much to see - two cribs about four feet by six feet took up the side walls and one small barred window was on the back wall. Apart from a small keg of water and a slops bucket under one of the cribs, there was nothing to see. The sleeping man snorted and rolled over.

Lawrie ran his hand over and under the wooden rail of the nearest crib and did the same to the other one, ignoring its inhabitant. They were all now watching Lawrie and giving each other quizzical looks as they wondered what he was doing. Aaron shrugged.

"What the hell Lawrie?" said Riley now completely bemused.

Finally, Lawrie stopped and grinned at them. "Back in London I had quite the reputation as a lock pick," he said continuing to run his hands over the underside of the crib.

"A lock pick?" scoffed Riley. "Yer a bloody ploughman from Belfast yer idiot. What do yer mean yer were a fuckin' lock pick in London?"

"Hush," said Paddy waving his arms about. "They'll hear yer."

"Just what I said," he said grinning. "I'm looking for a splinter of wood or something ter use ter pick that lock." He grabbed the padlock in his hand and looked closely at it. "It's a barrel lock, it'll be easy."

"Are yer serious?" said Riley getting to his feet and joining him. He peered at the lock and then at Lawrie. "Can yer really do it?"

Lawrie grinned and nodded. "I reckon."

"We should wait til that lot fall asleep tonight then we'll break outta here an' surprise them," said Riley indicating down the hall with his chin where they could hear the four soldiers and constable.

"Aye good idea, but I still need ter find something ter use as a pick."

"Yer heard him, lads," said Riley turning to the others. "There must be somethin' in here he can use."

They all set to work in earnest searching the small cell for anything that Lawrie could use. The sleeping man awoke with a fright when Paddy poked him in the side.

"Move we need ter search this crib."

"Huh what?" he said sitting up and peering bleary-eyed at his new companions.

"Move yer great lump," repeated Paddy shoving him aside.

"Ye'll have ter excuse, Paddy, there," said Riley shrugging. "So what's yer name an' what are yer doin' here?"

"Mick," the man replied rubbing his eyes. "Mick Cassidy an' I don't reckon it's any of yer business."

"Aye fair enough. I'm Patrick Riley, yer can call me Riley. An' this is Lawrie, Aaron an' Tom," said Riley pointing each of them out. "Of course yer already met Paddy."

"Aye," said Mick. "What are yer lot doin' then?"

"Well we're plannin' ter break outta here afore they send us downriver," said Riley. "Lawrie there just needs somethin' ter pick that lock with an' tonight we'll be breakin' out. Are yer with us?"

Mick rubbed his hands through his greying hair and nodded. "Maybe. What exactly are yer plannin'?"

"Revenge mostly," replied Riley matter of factly. "The first thing I'm goin' ter do if we git outta here is take care of James Reid. We should have done it days ago."

"Reid the bastard," said Mick. "He's the one who put me in here. Aye, count me in."

Riley grinned at him.

"How about this?" said Tom holding up a small length of wire.

"Perfect. Where'd yer get it?" said Lawrie taking it from him and straightening it out between his fingers. It was pliable but stiff enough to pick the lock.

"Twas holdin' the handle on the slops bucket where it's broke," said Tom looking pleased with himself.

~

Aaron had no idea what time it was, but the soldiers had gone quiet several hours ago. He could hear rhythmic breathing and soft snores coming from the end of the hall indicating they'd all gone to sleep. He smiled to himself. Idiots.

A slither of moonlight was coming into the small cell through the window and he hoped it'd be enough for Lawrie to see what he was doing. He'd been busy with the lock for at least ten minutes and Aaron didn't know how long it was going to take. He sat on the crib with the others and waited. His muscles were tense as he poised himself ready to pounce on their unsuspecting gaolers. Time ticked by and they all seemed to be holding their breath as Lawrie worked on the lock.

Half an hour later the click of metal and clinking of chain proved that Lawrie had succeeded. He removed the chain from the door and pushed it open with a creak before turning and grinning at them.

"Come on lads," he whispered.

They quietly crept from the cell and down the short hall. Aaron's heart was thumping madly as he followed. He could see the dark shapes of the men in front of him in the faint glow coming from the guard room. All of a sudden Riley stopped and gestured to Aaron and Paddy.

"Yer two take the two ahead in the guard room, the others must be in the bunk room," he whispered before turning and pushing Tom and Lawrie ahead of him into the small room on the left.

Without hesitating, Paddy and Aaron rushed into the guard room. In the faint light emanating from the glowing embers of the fire Aaron could see two soldiers slumped in chairs; asleep. Their weapons were lying beside them. He grabbed Paddy by the arm and pointed to the guns as he mouthed 'grab them'. Paddy nodded. They were about to put this plan into action when all hell let loose in the bunk room. Men started shouting and thumping and the two sleeping soldiers immediately woke up and leapt to their feet.

Although bleary-eyed with sleep, the one nearest to Aaron let out a yell and launched himself at him. He sidestepped but the man's flailing fist caught him in the side of the head. He stumbled, grabbing his head as he imagined his right ear already swelling like a cauliflower. The soldier was on him again before he had a chance to gather his wits and landed another blow in his side. Aaron yelped but rammed his elbow back into the man's soft belly as hard as he could. He heard him grunt as the wind was knocked out of him and he collapsed on the floor.

"I got him," said Mick who'd grabbed one of the muskets which he was now pointing at the man's chest. "Are yer awright?"

"Aye," said Aaron panting and placing a well-aimed kick in the soldier's ribs. "Bastard." His head was throbbing and there was a sharp pain in his ribs but he didn't think he was badly hurt.

Paddy had already subdued the other soldier who was lying on the floor groaning, holding his face. He'd slammed his face into his knee breaking his nose; blood was oozing down his face and smeared all over Paddy's jacket.

"Put yer hands where I can see them," said Paddy gesturing with the musket. "We've got these two, go an' see how Riley's going."

"Aye," said Aaron. He didn't get far as Riley appeared at the end of the hall.

"Everythin' awright? Have yer got them buggers?"

"Aye," said Aaron taking the rope he held out to him.

Before securing their captives they stripped them of most of their clothing and boots. They took their four muskets and ammunition along with a small supply of tobacco. The provisions the soldiers had mainly consisted of some hardtack, tea and sugar.

"Meagre supplies," said Lawrie screwing up his face. "We'll need ter get more guns and provisions first thing."

"Aye," agreed Riley throwing a musket over his shoulder. "Don't worry Lawrie we'll take care of it."

"Let's go," said Paddy casting a final look around the small barracks. "We need ter get outta here afore daybreak."

The six of them stepped out into the cold August night. It was a clear night with no cloud cover; the air was frigid and clouds of mist formed from their breath. Aaron thought it was probably about four in the morning, and they would have several hours before daybreak. He shivered as they made their way down the road towards the river.

His heart sank as they passed a house with several horses stabled in a small yard. Riley and Lawrie were already scaling the fence and encouraging the beasts towards them. Shit! He'd hoped he'd never have to get on the back of another one of those. In no time at all the two had seized saddles and bridles from a small tack room and had them saddled up and ready to ride. They led them out of the paddock and mounted up. Lawrie held his hand out to Aaron and he groaned, but resignedly swung up onto the back of the beast.

He had to hang on for dear life as Lawrie kicked the animal into a canter, and they careened down the road. Riley who was in the lead headed left before the river and down a steep embankment and over the Wallis Creek. The small settlement of Wallis Plains quickly gave way to almost impenetrable bush. The horses slowed to a walk as Riley picked out a wallaby track to follow westward. Tom was riding with Riley and it appeared to Aaron that he was giving him directions.

The quiet morning air was broken only by the thud of hooves on the narrow track as they continued on for several miles. Aaron finally relaxed his grip on Lawrie and sighed. He hoped they were heading for the hut on Spark's property that Tom had mentioned days ago. God, was that only two days ago? A lot seemed to have happened since then.

~

Chapter Eight

Wallis Plains, August 1825

Alexander Scott was generally up at dawn ready to face the day, but not today. After days in the saddle chasing down the bushrangers, he was exhausted and badly in need of rest. He never slept well out in the bush, not to mention that it had been pouring with rain and freezing cold. He was currently enjoying a rather pleasant dream whereby the Governor was thanking him personally for bringing in the outlaws.

Moments later he was rudely awoken by the loud banging on his door. This was followed by raised and urgent voices which appeared to be getting louder. His wife Maggie appeared at the bedroom door.

"Alexander you'll have to get up," she said, panic rising in her voice. "It's the bushrangers, they've escaped. Corporal Higgins said he came as soon as he could."

"What!" He leapt out of bed and rushed out the door still in his nightgown. Bloody hell! How could they have escaped? He'd already sent word to Sydney that he'd captured them. How was he going to explain this?

He met Corporal Higgins and three other soldiers in the hallway. He looked them up and down. What the hell? They weren't in uniform. They appeared to be wearing a very odd assortment of clothes that didn't match or fit very well. One of them looked like he'd had his face rammed in.

"What's the meaning of this Corporal? How could you have let them escape?"

"I'm sorry sir, but they caught us unawares and made off about an hour ago. We came as soon as we could."

Alexander compressed his lips and breathed in heavily through his nose. Idiots! "You have neglected your duty Corporal, and I'll take that matter up with your superior at a later date. Saddle my horse while I get dressed," he said angrily. "I hope you've got some idea which way they went?" he added over his shoulder. He didn't wait for an answer but marched back up the hall to his bedroom to dress.

Twenty minutes later he mounted his horse and set off in pursuit of them. He had no trackers and didn't hold much hope that Higgins had any clue which way to go. He had no choice but to try and find them. He was furious as he galloped down the road towards the river with the soldiers at his heels.

~

Riley came to a halt and Tom jumped down off the back of his horse. They were amongst a stand of large cedar trees with thick underbrush of grevilleas and bottlebrush. Aaron wondered why they'd stopped until he spied a small hut hidden amongst the trees. Without a word he silently slid off the back of the horse. God, he hoped to never get on another one as long as he lived. His limbs felt stiff and sore and he had a dull ache in his head where that damned soldier had hit him.

The others dismounted and they cautiously approached the hut. It looked like it had been deserted for some time. The roof had collapsed in one corner and the timber veranda was rotten in places, but otherwise, it looked like the perfect hideout. Riley cautiously stepped onto the veranda and pushed the door open. He turned and grinned at them.

"This will do nicely lads," he said as he disappeared inside.

Aaron grabbed a musket and followed him inside. It was a one-roomed hut without any furniture at all. There was a small fireplace which appeared to be in working order. They would at least be warm if not dry. The roof had obviously been leaking. A damp musty smell permeated the place, but it was going to be far better than camping under a rock or in a muddy cave. They grabbed the firearms and clothing that they'd taken from soldiers and let the horses go. Aaron was relieved about that.

They spent the next day resting and planning their next move. Riley wanted to attack Reid as soon as possible.

"I don't want ter miss another chance," he said vehemently.

"Aye you'll get yer chance," said Lawrie patiently. "But, first we need supplies an' weapons."

Paddy nodded. "I'm starving an' I'm sick ter death of hardtack. Let's go back an' pay Wilkins a visit. He'll have a good supply of provisions an' such."

"Aye," said Aaron agreeing with Paddy. Next to Reid, their old Overseer had to pay for his treatment of them. "I say we take care of Wilkins once and for all."

"I say we flog the bastard," put in Lawrie.

Tom and Mick didn't appear too concerned with their plans. Mick had made it clear he was with Riley when it came to Reid, but he seemed happy enough to wait for his chance. Riley finally conceded that they needed supplies first.

"Awright then. We'll pay Wilkins a visit tonight."

It was nearing eight o'clock by Aaron's estimation by the time they arrived at Jacob's farm. It was another clear moonlit night which promised a hard frost in the morning. They approached the overseer's hut with caution. There was no telling if Wilkins and his wife were home alone. The faint glow of lamplight could be seen through the window. Aaron sucked in a deep cold breath while they decided what to do.

"I reckon we just rush the joint," said Lawrie spitting a wad of tobacco. "Shoot the lock off the door an' surprise 'em good."

Riley nodded. "Aye," he said priming his musket. "Let's do it then."

Without another word, Riley started across the yard. The others quickly joined him and the six of them crept up to the veranda. Riley stepped cautiously onto it and then fired his musket. The lock was shattered by the blast and several splinters of wood peeled off the door frame. He immediately shoved his shoulder into the door and they all piled into the house.

Wilkins was seated at the kitchen table and looked up shocked and surprised by the intrusion. Without hesitation, he took to his heels out the back door. With a yell like a banshee, Lawrie gave chase, with

Tom right behind him. Mrs Wilkins just stared horrified at them. Aaron wondered if she was perhaps also shocked that her coward of a husband had just run off and left her. He was disgusted and hoped Lawrie would catch him. He very much wanted to see the bastard flogged.

"Well, well. Who do we have here?" said Paddy eyeing Mrs Wilkins' pretty face and slim figure.

She stared wide-eyed and backed away from him.

"Come now," he said coaxingly as he approached her. She glanced around, panic clear in her eyes as she looked for a way out. Before she could flee Paddy reached out a long arm and scooped her into his arms. He kissed her roughly, pinning her against the kitchen dresser.

Aaron turned away and ignored them. He may not agree with what Paddy was doing, but he wasn't about to interfere. He and the others began searching the house for weapons and other items. Wilkins had two muskets and a pistol which they took along with all his ammunition. The larder was well stocked and they helped themselves to pork, eggs and other staples.

Paddy dragged Mrs Wilkins out through the broken front door. She screamed and struggled against him, but he clapped a large hand over her mouth stifling her protests. Aaron watched them go and shrugged. Riley looked after them as well, but also didn't appear inclined to interfere. Aaron wondered if he was sorry Paddy had beaten him to it.

The others were busy wrapping their supplies in blankets to carry back to their hut when Lawrie and Tom arrived back.

"The bastard got away," said Lawrie dispassionately. "Bloody coward."

"Aye," said Riley. "Always knew he was a coward."

"We best not hang around," said Tom looking nervous. "Ye can bet he's gone for help."

"Aye, we'll have ter get supper elsewhere," said Mick. "I don't want ter hang around here an' get caught."

"Let's go then," said Lawrie picking up a load of supplies. "Where's Paddy?"

Riley gave Lawrie a queer look. "Outside. Probably in the barn."

Lawrie raised an eyebrow at him. "The barn?"

"I'll go fetch him."

A few minutes later Riley returned with Paddy in tow. They gathered up their loot and left heading south. They crossed the river and turned west towards Spark's and their hut. Aaron's stomach grumbled. He was starving and wondered when he might get supper. He wasn't the only one thinking about food as they dropped their supplies off at the hut.

"I could eat a horse," said Paddy grumbling. "I say we go back ter that last farmhouse we passed an' get some supper."

"That'd be Winder's place," said Tom nodding in agreement. "His overseer's a real bastard from what I hear."

"Really?" said Riley, his interest clearly piqued. "Well, perhaps we ought ter pay him a visit then."

After further discussion, they all agreed to raid Winder's overseer. Aaron and Tom would dress in the soldier's uniforms they'd stolen from the barracks. They'd pretend to be bringing in some captured bushrangers requiring shelter for the night. Aaron put the jacket and hat on and swung a musket over his shoulder. He grinned at Tom as the pair now looked like bona fide red-coats.

"Alright, so who's going to be the captured bushrangers?" asked Aaron eyeing the rest of them.

"Oh me," said Lawrie enthusiastically jumping to his feet.

Paddy grinned at him and agreed to be the other one. He held his hands out and Riley bound them and then Lawrie's.

They stepped out into the cold night air which was already moist with dew. The shrubs and bushes were wet with it. They marched along a narrow wallaby track back towards Winder's. Aaron thought it must be well past midnight, and he wondered briefly how many might be sleeping in the house. Tom didn't think the overseer was married, but it was likely that other men would be housed with him. He was feeling nervous as they approached the house, and he sucked in a couple of calming deep breaths. Alright, this was it – he hoped the ruse would work.

Aaron gave one last glance over his shoulder. Riley and Mick were well out of sight. Tom had his musket pointing directly at Lawrie and Paddy, who were standing behind him, their heads bowed. He took another breath and hammered loudly on the door.

He waited until he heard the thump of footsteps coming from inside the house before he yelled out. "Corporal Brown and Private Smith at your service. We've got two outlaws."

A moment later the door was swung open by a short sallow man wearing a dark jacket over his nightshirt. He peered at Aaron momentarily before taking a step back to allow him entry.

"I 'spect I can put ye an' ye prisoners up in the barn for the night," he said turning his back.

He was reaching to light an oil lamp when Aaron jammed the muzzle of his musket into his back. "Let me see your hands."

"What the hell are ye about?" he asked indignantly, although he had quickly complied by raising his hands.

Tom rushed into the house behind Aaron along with Lawrie and Paddy. He quickly cut their ropes before heading into the other room to flush out any other inhabitants. Lawrie stuck his head out the door and called to Riley and Mick. Meanwhile, Paddy secured the man by tying his hands behind his back and shoving him into a chair.

A moment later Tom returned with two more men in their nightclothes at gunpoint. They goggled at the intruders but recognition seemed to shine in their eyes. Aaron suspected that news of their escape had already reached the settlers, and a pursuit party was probably already out after them.

"I found this pair in there," said Tom indicating to the other room. "Ain't no one else."

Riley nodded while Lawrie and Aaron grabbed them roughly and tied them up as well. "Sit down an' shut up an' yer won't git hurt," said Riley brandishing a large hunting knife.

Aaron opened the damper on the fire and tossed a couple of logs on it. He hoped

Paddy would get supper started. He was right. Paddy set to searching the larder and began preparing eggs and pork. Aaron found several bottles of wine and set them on the table. His stomach grumbled noisily as the smell of frying pork filled the air; he was starving.

"Ye won't get away with this," spat Winder's overseer. "Scott's already ert after ye an' he'll see ye hanged."

"Shut it," said Riley glaring at the man. "Or I'll make yer shut it."

He glared back at Riley and breathed heavily through his nose in an obvious attempt to keep quiet. Aaron wondered what Riley might have in mind for the man if he persisted. He shrugged.

Tom and Mick were already ransacking the small house for weapons and ammunition. They found a pair of pistols along with another musket. The larder was well stocked with provisions which they stacked near the door. This included a cask of salt pork, flour, oats and tea; enough for several days.

They spent the next few hours eating and drinking until Aaron thought he couldn't eat another bite. He groaned as he pushed his chair back from the table. The wine was making him feel self-confident and sure of himself, and perhaps a little brash. The doubts he'd had earlier when they were captured had all but evaporated.

He eyed Winder's overseer who was slumped in the chair they'd tossed him in. He was disappointed they hadn't flogged Wilkins earlier, and he was getting anxious. He desperately wanted to take his frustration out on someone. All this breaking into houses and stealing stuff was alright, but where was it all going? He took a large gulp of wine and gestured with his chin towards the man.

"What are we going to do about him?"

The others looked at him and then to the overseer. Lawrie shrugged and went back to his wine. Tom and Mick exchanged interested looks.

"What did yer have in mind?" asked Paddy eyeing the man and then grinning at Aaron. "

"Well, I heard him earlier. He'd like to see us hanged."

"That he did," put in Riley showing some interest in the conversation.

"Well then," said Paddy getting to his feet. "I reckon we ought ter give him a taste of his own medicine. What do yer say, lads?"

None of them needed any further encouragement. They were all feeling the same frustration at Wilkins escaping their grasp. Paddy grabbed the man roughly and wrenched him to his feet.

"Come with us."

He yelped with fright at being manhandled. "Get off me!"

Aaron grabbed a length of rope from near the pile of items they planned to take and tied a rough noose. He threw one end over the rafters and put the noose over the overseer's head.

Paddy gave him a swift kick. "Get on the chair."

"I won't tell anyone ye was here. I swear," he said his eyes bugging out of his head in terror. "Please."

The other two men stared horrified at the proceedings but said nothing. They were clearly hoping the bushrangers wouldn't turn their attention to them.

"Get on the chair," repeated Paddy impatiently.

"No – please I swear. I'm sorry 'bout what I said earlier. Please."

Lawrie grabbed the man on the other side and he and Paddy heaved him onto the chair and secured the rope.

"I suggest yer don't fall off that chair," said Riley smirking. "Come on lads let's get outta here."

They grabbed the supplies and weapons and Aaron gave the house one last glance as he stepped out in the early morning. The overseer was standing on the chair looking terrified, while the others were staring open-mouthed. He suspected they'd free him soon enough; before he fell off the chair. He shut the door and left.

~

Chapter Nine

Wallis Plains, August 1825

It was nearly dawn by the time the gang made their way back to the hut. They were exhausted and spent the next few days resting and sleeping. Riley was anxious to strike Reid's place, but the rest of them convinced him to conduct some reconnaissance first. They didn't want to get chased off again. He'd finally agreed and Lawrie and Tom had gone first thing this morning to check the place out.

Aaron yawned and stretched. He was glad the others had decided to rest for a few days. He'd been bone-weary by the time they'd left Winder's overseer's house the other night. He briefly wondered if the man had hung himself or not. He didn't care – from all accounts he was a mean bastard who deserved all he got.

"Someone's comin'," said Mick who'd positioned himself by the window to keep an eye out "It's awright – it's Tom an' Lawrie. They got someone with them."

Aaron, Paddy and Riley peered out. Sure enough, it was Lawrie and Tom with another man - obviously a convict by his garb. Riley opened the door and called out to them.

"Who yer got there?"

"Tis awright," said Lawrie grinning at him "This is John McDonnell. He's one of McLeod's. We ran into him on our way back from Reid's."

"Aye," he said eyeing the man.

John stopped outside the hut and looked warily back at Riley. "I've run off ter join yer lot."

He was about the same height as Lawrie with straight light brown hair which he'd pulled back in a queue. Aaron thought the more men that joined them the better. If there were enough of them they could really put fear into the likes of James Reid.

"An' why would yer want ter do that? We'll likely hang if we git caught," said Riley still standing in the doorway.

John nodded. "Aye, an' I hear Scott's livid that yer got away. He's been ert lookin' for yer with soldiers. He came by yesterday an' stayed the night at McLeod's."

"Did he really? Has he got trackers?"

"He didn't, but he might have now."

Lawrie pushed past Riley and went into the hut. "Enough questions Riley, he's fine."

Riley stepped back into the hut and gestured to John to enter. "Awright yer can join us," he said shrugging. "So what about Reid?" he said turning to Lawrie. "What did yer find out?"

"Well we found a good spot ter spy on him," said Tom grinning. "There's a great fig-tree not far from his house an' we watched him from there."

Lawrie lifted the lid of the billy and peered in. "Aye. It gave us a good idea."

"An' what was that?" said Riley raising an eyebrow.

"We reckon we should set fire to his house an' barn," said Lawrie grinning. "We'd be able ter watch it burn from the great fig tree."

A wide smile spread over Riley's face. "Aye. When?"

"So this morning he sent all the croppies off with his overseer, an' then he an' his wife an' children went off as well," said Lawrie.

"Aye," put in Tom. "I expect the same will happen again tomorrow. But we can go an' watch an' make sure."

"I'm all for it," said Mick grinning. "I can't wait for that bastard to get his."

"Awright, I'll come with yer in the mornin' ter see for meself," said Riley.

"We should all go," put in Aaron. "Are you sure they won't see us hiding in the tree?"

"No. It's a huge tree," said Lawrie tipping the tea into the boiling water. "It's the perfect hiding spot."

~

The seven of them set off for Reid's in the early hours of the morning. It was a freezing cold night and the heavy dew was already starting to set into a hard frost. Aaron wrapped the blanket more firmly around his shoulders as they trudged through the bush to Reid's farm. They crossed the river and followed it eastward, skirting around McLeod and Jacob's properties.

They stopped for a brief rest by a fallen log. Aaron hunched down beside it and glanced around. The undergrowth was sparse among the tall river gums and all around was quiet. He sighed; his misty breath hanging in the air in front of him.

"It's not far ter Reid's from here," said Lawrie munching on a hard biscuit. "We'll be there afore daybreak."

Riley nodded. "I can't wait til we git that bastard."

The others murmured their agreement with Riley. Aaron was of the same mind. They needed to do something more than just break in and steal stuff. He wanted their former masters to be afraid; wanted very much for them to be on edge, not knowing when they might strike next. Setting fire to Reid's house would send just the right message. He was anxious to get on with it.

The quiet morning air was shattered with the sound of musket fire, quickly followed by men yelling. Aaron leapt to his feet along with the others. He scanned the bush before taking to his heels heading west. Lawrie was ahead of him as they went crashing through the bush. His heart was hammering; he had no idea how many there were, or how far behind they might be.

He heard a shot nearby and glanced sideways in time to see Riley put his musket to his shoulder and fire. "It's Scott an' he's got soldiers with him," he panted shouldering his weapon.

"Run," yelled Paddy as he ran passed them. "Red-coats!"

Aaron paused for the briefest moment before tearing through the bush after him. They headed for higher ground where the undergrowth was thicker and would provide some cover. He was panting heavily and his legs were screaming for him to stop as they ran up the hill from the river. Riley and Mick were right behind them as the five of them dived behind a rocky outcrop. Riley proceeded to reload his musket, while Aaron put his gun to his shoulder ready to fire if he saw any sign of their pursuers. Paddy and Lawrie had their weapons aimed down the hill as well, while Mick had his pistol cocked ready.

Aaron sucked in several large lungfuls of air as he peered into the bush; poised, every muscle tensed as he waited. They sat there scanning the bush for several minutes before they realised they weren't being pursued.

"Shit," said Riley finally putting his musket by his side. "They must've got Tom an' John."

"Damn," said Aaron coming to the same realisation. That's obviously why they weren't pursuing them. "Why didn't we hear them coming sooner? Do you reckon they were following us?"

"I dunno," said Paddy breathing heavily as he tried to catch his breath. "Bastards."

"Yer can be sure of one thing," said Lawrie dispassionately. "They ain't gonna turn their backs on 'em an' let 'em escape."

Aaron had to agree. Scott wouldn't be so foolish again. He'd have them well guarded and shackled so there'd be no chance of them escaping.

They waited and listened for a good hour before they finally crept out from behind the outcrop. All was quiet as they headed back down the hill towards the river. Aaron glanced sideways and paused to turn and look behind. He was nervous. It seemed likely to him that Scott might still be out searching for the rest of them. He would've liked to lay low for the day and return to their hut later that night, but Riley was intent on getting back.

"We'll need ter rest so we can head off for Reid's again in the early hours," he said. "I will not wait any longer ter git my revenge on him."

Aaron shrugged. He was hard pressed not to agree with him.

~

Alexander Scott had mixed feelings. On the one hand, he was delighted they'd captured two of the bushrangers, but he was furious with McCain. He'd told them to hold their fire until they were well on the outlaws, but the idiot had panicked and fired. He was bloody lucky they'd caught any of them under the circumstances.

He was determined these two would be despatched to Sydney with all haste. He wouldn't be giving them any opportunity to escape this time. He rode along to the solid thump of hooves on the packed earth. The two prisoners were stumbling ahead of him, shackled and chained together. As far as he was concerned, they would remain that way until they'd been received in Sydney. He had no desire to try and explain another escape to the Governor.

He would need to set off in pursuit of the rest of them as soon as possible. He relaxed in the saddle as they plodded along. He planned to leave the two prisoners in Corporal Higgins custody. Surely the idiot could be trusted to secure them in the barracks and keep them there until they could be sent to Newcastle. Then he could get on with the job of capturing the rest of them. He'd impose upon McLeod for fresh horses and men – he could hardly refuse him under the circumstances. He wondered if he could get hold of the native trackers as well. Either way, he'd be back in pursuit before the end of the day.

~

In the early hours of the following morning, the five remaining outlaws left their hut and headed for James Reid's property. Their plan was simple enough. Wait for Reid and his family to leave the house and then set fire to it. They were each carrying hot embers from their fire wrapped in moss and bark.

It was daybreak when they arrived at Reid's farm and Lawrie led them to the hiding spot that he and Tom had found a couple of days before. The giant fig tree was on a slight rise, its huge branches extending skyward. Its trunk appeared to be many trunks and formed a curtain like barrier large enough to conceal the five men.

From their hiding spot, Aaron could clearly see the farmhouse with the barn behind it. They'd have no trouble seeing when the house and yard were deserted. He also noticed a large field of wheat on the other side of the barn. He nudged Riley and pointed it out.

"We ought to burn that as well."

"Aye," replied Riley surveying the scene. "Paddy an' me will take care of the house. Lawrie an' Aaron, you do the barn. Mick yer can take care of that field of wheat."

They all nodded in agreement. All they had to do now was wait.

Half an hour later they saw Reid emerge from the house. His overseer had assembled the work gangs for the day. They were standing in the yard waiting for instructions. Reid's voice floated to them, but Aaron couldn't make out what he was saying. He was gesturing and waving his arms about, and a few minutes later the overseer and convicts headed off.

Aaron, like the rest of them, was anxious for him to leave as well. He hoped they'd be able to burn his house to the ground, leaving nothing but charred remains. He sighed, as Reid disappeared back into the house.

Jacob's Mob

"He'll be back out in a minute or two," said Lawrie as if he was reading the question on Aaron's mind.

Aaron nodded and waited. He could already feel adrenalin starting to thrum through his veins with excitement. He removed the top piece of moss from his hot ember and breathed softly on it. It immediately glowed red. He smiled and covered it again. He had a pocket full of dry grass that he was confident would catch alight quickly when the time came.

Five minutes later Reid re-emerged from the house with a young boy by the hand and his wife by his side. She had a small child in one arm and a bucket in the other. They appeared to be chatting amiably as they went off in the same direction as the work gangs.

They waited for a few more minutes, watching the deserted yard just in case someone might come back. When they didn't Riley breathed a sigh.

"Awright lads, yer know what ter do," he said grinning at them. "Let's go."

Aaron immediately sprang to his feet and headed down to the barn with Lawrie by his side. They entered the dimly lit building which only had two small windows letting the light in. It took a moment for their eyes to adjust. It appeared that Reid was using the barn for storage. There were several bales of hay, saddles and bridles and a few farm implements in one corner. The rest of the barn was stacked with sacks of wheat. Aaron grabbed a handful of hay and stuffed it down beside the back wall and under the sacks of wheat. Lawrie was busy doing the same.

Aaron took his hot ember and placed it down beside the hay and blew softly on it until it caught fire. He quickly did the same thing in several other places before he and Lawrie headed for the door. He set a small fire beside that as well before they left.

They came out of the barn grinning at each other. Aaron glanced towards the wheat field behind the barn and smiled as he saw wisps of smoke already starting to curl into the morning air. He hoped the entire field would burn. They hurried back to the giant fig tree where they could watch the fire without being seen. Aaron didn't expect it would take long before Reid or his overseer noticed the rising smoke, but he hoped the house and barn would be well alight by then.

Riley and Paddy were the last ones to come back to the hideout. Riley grinned from ear to ear as the smoke began to billow in earnest and the sound of fire crackling the dry timber reached their ears. They'd lit small fires around the perimeter of the house which were now licking up the walls. In no time at all the dry timber house was ablaze and the rising smoke had been seen by Reid. Raised voices yelling 'fire' preceded the arrival of a dozen or so men.

Aaron spotted Reid's pale blonde head easily among the throng who came racing into the yard. He immediately went into the house and moments later came out dragging a sideboard. One of the other men joined him and helped drag it from the burning house. Others went inside and came out armed with blankets which they were using to try and stamp out the flames. Reid managed to drag several chairs out of the house which he dropped in the yard beside the other furniture.

His wife arrived with the children and even from this distance, Aaron could see the horror on her face. She screamed her husband's name as he made to go back into the house to rescue more of their belongings. He only made it as far as the veranda before the flames forced him back.

Aaron and the others watched with glee as the flames licked out of the windows and caught the veranda ablaze. There was no hope of putting it out. The barn was burning with equal ferocity. Aaron doubted they'd be able to save even one sack of wheat.

The gang watched from the shelter of the fig tree until the house was nothing but a pile of ash and charred remains. The wheat field had also been completely destroyed and Aaron thought the barn would smoulder for days. It was well after midday before they left their hidey-hole and headed back to their hut. Riley was humming as they trudged through the bush towards Spark's property. Aaron smiled. Justice had been served.

~

Chapter Ten

Donald McLeod's Homestead

Don McLeod took in a deep breath and sighed. His homestead was crowded with his neighbours who were all trying to talk at once. Some of them were getting rather loud and Standish Harris had just thumped his large meaty fist into his dining table. The fear amongst them concerning the bushrangers had reached a fever pitch. Not that he blamed them. He was thankful they hadn't robbed his home or burnt it to the ground for that matter.

"Who's going to protect us if not ourselves?" Standish was now shouting. "We need a proper night watch."

"Aye we do, and I'd happily volunteer, but who's going to protect my home and wife while I'm out on watch?" said William Hicks breathing heavily. "You know they terrorised my wife and made her cook them supper! It was an outrage."

Several of them nodded, and there were murmurs of agreement. It was beyond belief that the outlaws were committing such outrages. Don ran his fingers through his hair as he eyed his neighbours. He knew they were worried, but they seemed more concerned about themselves than the larger problem. Surely the good Lieutenant knew they'd committed much worse atrocities against others than forcing their wives to cook them supper. For God sake, they'd burnt Reid's homestead to the ground.

"Gentlemen, we must stand together if we hope to bring an end to these outlaws," said Don trying to appeal their better natures. "Vicars Jacob's overseer, Dan Wilkins, has resigned and returned to Sydney. I myself have had to muster his croppies until he arranges a replacement."

There was a murmur through the men as they all turned and stared at Don. Some, including Dr Evans, looked accusingly at him.

"But it's his damn convicts that are on the loose," said William Evans indignantly. "What's he doing about it? And why has his damn overseer taken off in such a way?" His anger and frustration was unmistakable.

"Did you not hear?" put in David Mazicre. "They dragged his wife off and did unspeakable things." He shook his head solemnly. "You cannot blame the man."

Evans goggled at him mouth agape. "No I did not hear," he said shutting his mouth abruptly.

"We need action. None of us are safe in our beds," said Standish Harris.

"Jacob's has got to do something," added William Evans lamely.

"I agree with Dr Evans," put in James Reid. "But my wife is terrified and I'll be taking her to stay with her sister in Parramatta at the first opportunity."

No one was going to argue with James Reid taking his family to safety in Parramatta. They all knew too well that his house had been burnt to the ground. It was for that very reason that they'd gathered today to deal with the growing boldness of the outlaws. God only knew what they'd do next.

"Mr Scott has already captured two of them," said Don McLeod trying to move the conversation away from blame and onto doing something. "I'm confident he'll have the rest of them in custody any day now."

Once again there were some murmurs of agreement amongst them so he pressed on. "Scott can't pursue bushrangers and protect our farms as well. We must stand together gentlemen. I propose we put together a night watch to protect our women and homes."

He was pleased to see that even those who were posturing and full of wind quieted and begrudgingly murmured agreement. It was paramount that they protect their families, they all knew that. He took a deep breath.

"I still say Jacob's should be doing more," said William Evans refusing to let the matter go. "Where is he anyway?"

"Safe in Sydney with his family I expect, and he's got no reason to come here," said Standish Harris. "Why would he?"

"Well, he's going to have to appoint a new overseer. Surely he doesn't expect you to take responsibility for his croppies.

Does he?" said Hicks turning to Don, outrage on his face.

Don honestly had no idea what Jacob's expected of him and his neighbours. He certainly hadn't sent any word on what he intended to do, or when a new overseer might be arriving.

He sighed and shrugged. "I don't know."

This gave them more reason to debate the merits of Vicars Jacob and his convicts further. The majority of them appeared happy to find someone to blame, and that was Jacob's. Don took a deep breath and waited for them to finish their arguments once more. The conversation wasn't going in the direction he was hoping for at all. Finally, they all quieted enough for him to interject.

"Gentlemen, if we could just agree to all post a night watch. We need to stop them from getting fresh supplies and stealing more firearms," he said exasperated. "It is to all of our advantages to cut off supply."

They nodded and murmured agreement, and even Dr Evans agreed with cutting off supply. Don just wasn't sure if Evans was prepared to do anything himself.

"Don's right," said Standish finally conceding. "We can all post a watch and hopefully cut off supplies."

"Aye. In the meantime, we can only hope Mr Scott catches the rest of them buggers," put in Maziere. "Has anyone heard from him?"

"He called in here a few days ago for fresh horses," said Don pleased to be able to update them on the pursuit. "He thinks they're being kept very well informed by the croppies and others. At the moment they appear to be two steps ahead of him I'm afraid."

"I heard some croppies had items the mob had stolen. Do you really think they're helping them?" said William Hicks, fear and concern etched on his face.

"Well of course they are," scoffed Dr Evans.

"Let's be honest gentlemen. Only one in fifty convicts would stand on our side, the rest are no doubt relishing the chaos the bushrangers are causing," said Don. He had no doubt where his own convict's allegiance lay, and it wasn't with him.

"What about the natives?" said Alexander Spark, who'd been quiet up until this point. "Has Scott got trackers?"

Don shook his head. "He did initially, but for some reason, the natives are no longer co-operating. "

"Hrm," said Alexander Spark. "That's rather odd don't you think?"

"I do," said Don shrugging. He honestly had no idea why they'd not only stopped tracking for them, but were nowhere to be found. It was like they'd just disappeared. Of course, they hadn't; they were just very good at concealing themselves and not being found if they didn't want to be.

He suspected it had something to do with Reid's house being burned down. He privately thought the natives might consider the bushrangers to be allies. If they continued to burn the settlers out then that could only be to their advantage. Not that it would drive the settlers away for any length of time, but he thought the natives might have thought so.

"So, gentlemen are we in agreement?" said Don wanting to be sure they all understood what was required. "Each of us will post an armed night watch in an attempt to cut off supply."

There were nods and murmurs of agreement and Don sighed with relief. His wife Ann entered with a tray of refreshments for their guests which also helped to put an end to further arguments. By the time they all left Don was feeling confident that the bushrangers would be starved out if Scott didn't catch them – and he was sure Scott would catch them.

~

Alexander Scott held the mug of tea between his freezing fingers. He squatted down by the smoky fire trying to get some warmth into his bones. They'd been out looking for the outlaws for a week or more and he was exhausted. He groaned as he sat back on his haunches. The rain was continuing to drizzle which was making him even more miserable. He pulled his hat down further over his ears and sighed.

"Private McCain's got the horses saddled an' ready to go," said George McIntire squatting down by the fire beside him. "I reckon the weather might clear later on."

Alexander cast his eyes skyward. It was grey and overcast with no sign of blue or of the sun trying to get through. "Maybe," he mumbled taking a large sip of the hot tea. He felt it warm him all the way down his gullet and he sighed. He'd have to call off the search if they didn't catch up to the bushrangers today. He couldn't afford to spend any more time searching for them.

George got to his feet and began packing his saddlebags. Alexander cast a look in his direction. He was McLeod's man, and he was grateful that he'd sent him along, but he was no match for Mullabuy. He gulped down the last of his tea and stood up. He stretched and began packing his own bags. It would be another long day in the saddle.

Half an hour later they mounted up and continued the search. Scott had no idea where they might be. He'd spent days scouring the bush along the Wallis Creek, and two days ago they'd headed inland into higher ground. They'd seen no sign that they'd been in this part of the country.

They picked their way down hill through rough country following a wallaby track. Alexander thought they might be camping on the other side of the river. It would be riskier, closer to Wallis Plains but he'd come up empty-handed everywhere else. The rain was getting heavier and a chilling wind was blowing its icy fingers under his collar. He shivered and urged his horse to quicken its pace. The sooner he got back to Wallis Plains and his own fireplace the better.

~

Chapter Eleven

Aaron spooned the last morsel of porridge in his mouth, sat back and sighed. He would've liked a mug of hot tea, but there wasn't any. In fact, most of their supplies were depleted and they'd need to raid a farmhouse for more; probably today.

"I reckon we'll need ter go further afield for supplies," said Lawrie stretching. "The nearest farms will no doubt be on the lookout for us."

Riley nodded in agreement as he finished his own porridge.

"We're gonna need ter get more supplies today," put in Paddy grumbling. "We got no tea, no sugar an' that's the last of the oats."

"We could do with some dry clothes as well," put in Mick.

The wet weather had returned and although they'd been hiding out in their hut, it was damp and leaky. Much of their bedding was wet and their clothes had a damp feeling about them. The whole hut had an unwholesome damp and musty smell about it. Aaron screwed up his nose in distaste.

"Awright we'll go an' git fresh supplies an' such," said Riley. "But I agree with Lawrie, we'll need ter go a little further east."

"Gather yer weapons lads. Ain't no time like now," said Paddy slinging a musket over his shoulder and shoving a pistol in his belt.

"Aye," said Aaron grinning at him. He likewise picked up a musket and grabbed some shot and powder. He wrapped a blanket over his shoulders. It was damp and smelled a bit mouldy but he didn't care. It would be cold and wet outside.

Lawrie shoved a couple of Johnny cakes in his pocket and handed two to Aaron. "Yer might get hungry afore we get more supplies."

"Aye," he replied putting the cakes in the pocket of his jacket and following Mick and Riley out the door.

There was a bit of light rain in the air which wasn't too much of a concern. Only a slight breeze was blowing which Aaron was relieved about. When the icy winds blew they chilled him to the bone. They headed off towards Wallis Plains keeping to a well-used wallaby track until they crossed the river.

They followed the river around past McLeod and Jacob's properties. They were well aware that Wilkins had left following their last visit. They crept close enough to check out their old overseer's house. It looked deserted. Aaron wondered how long it would take for Jacob's to arrange for a new overseer. He shrugged. He didn't care, except it was easy to raid for provisions.

They continued on, skirting around Hicks property so they could take a good look at Reid's burnt out homestead. No one was around, and the remains looked like charred skeletons. Aaron noticed Riley and Mick looked particularly pleased with the result. They continued eastward leaving the river behind.

Another half a mile or so on they came to a creek which they followed north to William Evans farm. It was a large property, with a substantial looking homestead situated not far from the creek.

As they approached a window at the front of the house opened and the muzzle of a gun appeared. Aaron stopped dead, as did the others. They'd all seen the window open. He half expected a shot to come whizzing by his ear, but it didn't.

Evans had hesitated and Riley was undaunted.

"Put the gun down an' open the door," he called out.

"Take one more step and I'll shoot."

"You're outnumbered," said Riley looking around at his men. "Open the door an' put the gun down or we'll set yer house on fire."

"Aye, don't think we won't," yelled Paddy confidently. "Yer would've heard what we did ter Reid."

Evan's didn't shoot, but he didn't give any ground either. His musket was still pointing directly at Riley's chest. Aaron wondered how this impasse was going to end. They hadn't brought any hot coals with them, and he didn't have a flint and stone. Lawrie might have one, otherwise setting fire to his house was an empty threat. He suspected Evans might think so as well.

Before he could consider this further, however, he heard voices coming. His heart started thumping madly with alarm. Shit, someone was coming. Riley and the others had heard them as well. They had no time to head for cover, so armed themselves ready to fire upon whoever was approaching.

"I suggest you leave now while you still can," called William Evans.

Aaron stood his ground with the others, his musket at his shoulder ready to fire. He could feel the adrenalin coursing through him and fear gripped his belly; he sucked in several deep breaths as he stood there poised. The voices were getting louder and he expected whoever it was to break cover any minute.

Eight men wearing convict slops emerged from out of the acacia trees heading for the house. They stopped; surprise clear on their faces when they saw the bushrangers. One of them, a large barrel-chested man looked from them to the house and back again, before a wide grin spread across his face.

"Are ye Jacob's mob then?"

"Aye," said Riley warily.

"You're the outnumbered ones," yelled Evans from the house. "Leave while you still can."

The man looked briefly towards the house but ignored Evans. "Do ye plan on ransacking the place?"

Riley flexed his fingers on his musket. Aaron wasn't yet sure whose side the croppies would take, and Riley wasn't either.

"Aye," he said once more, still not relaxing his grip on the gun.

Another wide grin spread across the man's face. "Well lads, looks like we've come just in time," he said turning to his fellow convicts.

"Come up to the house Wilson," called Evans. "I'll let you in. I've got more muskets."

The rest of the convicts smiled at Wilson and nodded, but none of them made a move towards the house. "I think not," Wilson called out to his master. "After all tis, not our fight."

Riley took in a large breath and grinned. "So, twould seem yer badly outnumbered," he called to Evans as he took a step towards the house. "Let us in or I'll burn yer out."

Aaron waited, poised, still with his musket at the ready. Would Evans open the door or fire at them? Surely he realised that he'd only get off one shot before they rushed the house. Still, he wasn't sure, and every muscle tensed as they waited. He breathed a massive of sigh of relief when the door opened and Dr William Evans stepped out onto his veranda. He glared at them, but he dropped his weapon and surrendered.

"Well lads," said Riley shouldering his musket and grinning at them. "Let's git some supplies."

They rushed into the house and began ransacking it for provisions, firearms and anything of value. It was a large homestead with several rooms including a well stocked larder. Aaron could hear Evans' croppies talking and laughing outside. He grinned.

"Hey Paddy give me a hand," he said grabbing a kitchen chair. "The croppies out there need something to sit on while they wait."

"Aye they do," said Paddy laughing. He grabbed a chair as well and they took them outside for the croppies. Mick grinned when he saw what they were doing and gave them a hand. Evans glared at them as they tossed his chairs from the veranda to the convicts.

"Here have a seat lads," said Aaron throwing the chair from the veranda. It landed in the mud in front of the large convict named Wilson. He laughed before righting it and sitting down.

"Thank ye."

Aaron went back into the house to help Lawrie get fresh supplies. When he entered the kitchen Lawrie already had a sack of flour and rice on the table.

"Is there any wine in there?" asked Aaron.

"No worse luck," he said putting a box of tea on the table. "There's everything else though."

Aaron shrugged. "Wine would've been nice," he picked up the flour and rice and headed off to the front door with them.

Riley emerged from the bedroom with blankets and a pocket watch. Paddy had muskets and ammunition and Mick had dressed himself in Dr Evan's best shirt and jacket.

"How'd I look," he said smirking and looking himself up and down.

"Like a toff," said Paddy grinning at him. "I'd best get some for meself," he said dropping the firearms and heading off to the bedroom.

Aaron and Mick bundled up the smaller items in a blanket making them easier to carry. By the time Paddy came back dressed in clean clothes belonging to Evans, they were loaded up and ready to go. Riley gave one more look over his shoulder as he walked out the front door. He grinned when he saw the croppies sitting on chairs in the front yard.

"Thank yer lads," he said. "Yer were a great help. Would yer mind restraining the good Doctor for a bit? Twould give us a chance to git away."

"Aye. We'll do our best to keep him here for a bit."

"Thank yer," said Paddy laughing as they headed off.

They needed to put some distance between William Evans and themselves before he could raise the alarm or inform his neighbours.

~

They planned to head straight back to their hut armed with sacks of flour, rice and sugar. They had enough provisions to last a couple of weeks and with the deteriorating weather, they planned to hole up for a few days. They were walking along in single file near Narrow Gut when Riley came to an abrupt halt. Ahead Aaron could see several natives; they appeared to be blocking their path.

He glanced at Lawrie, who shrugged. They'd never had any trouble with the natives. In fact, even on Jacob's land, there were never any problems with them. They tended to keep to themselves for the most part. He peered around Mick who was ahead of him to get a better look at them.

Jacob's Mob

There were three men wearing full-length animal skin cloaks and carrying spears. They didn't appear to be threatening, but nonetheless, Aaron's stomach clenched. He scanned the bush, half expecting to see red-coats, but he didn't see anyone else. Riley stood frozen on the path ahead. He hadn't loaded his musket or even attempted to protect himself. Aaron sucked in a deep breath and waited to see what they were going to do.

One of them stepped forward and addressed Riley. "Jacob's mob?"

"Aye. I'm Riley."

A wide smile spread across the native's face and he spoke to his companions. "Nganhanybula." *It's them.* They all grinned. "Me Birrani. Yarran an' Ngarra," he said gesturing to the others.

"Paddy, Mick, Aaron an' Lawrie," replied Riley pointing to each one of them.

Aaron relaxed and took a step forward. He'd never been so close to them before and he was curious. They were tall, and he thought they were slim under their cloaks which he noticed were decorated with different designs. They had broad

182

noses and deep-set eyes, and their faces had been painted with dots in different colours. He couldn't help but wonder what they wanted. And how did they know who they were? He shifted the sack of rice he was carrying onto his other shoulder.

"We no hunt you anymore. Or Mullabuy," said Birrani his face serious.

Aaron took this to mean that they were no longer tracking for the soldiers. He grinned and gave Mick a nudge. "That's good news."

Mick turned his head and shrugged.

"Thank yer," said Riley nodding and smiling at Birrani.

"You set more fires," said Birrani grinning. Ngarra and Yarran nodded their heads and grinned as well.

Aaron couldn't see Riley's face, but he jerked his head and Aaron thought he was surprised by this. It dawned on him that the reason the natives were no longer tracking them was because they'd burnt Reid's house down. Did they expect them to burn more of the settler's out? He thought so. Still, this had to be good news, didn't it? The soldiers would have no hope of finding them without the native trackers. A wide smile spread across Aaron's face.

"We ought to co-operate with them," he whispered to Riley. "They could be very helpful."

Riley nodded. Paddy shot Aaron a look that clearly said he thought the idea preposterous.

"We might light more fires," said Riley relaxing somewhat. "Come with us back ter our camp."

Paddy looked at Riley alarmed. "Are yer mad?"

"We're on the same side," said Riley putting his hand on Paddy's forearm. "Come with us. It's not far," he repeated shifting his load of provisions.

Birrani turned to his companions and spoke to them in their own strange language. They were obviously conferring and deciding whether to come with them or not. Yarran looked warily at them, but Ngarra shrugged and appeared to think it was a good idea.

"Aye," said Birrani at last and the three stepped aside to let Riley go first.

Riley continued down the rough track towards their hut. Birrani fell in behind him followed by Paddy. The other two natives followed at the rear. Aaron could hear Riley up ahead chatting with Birrani. He thought the young native was describing the countryside as they walked. He was waving his arms about and appeared to be pointing out various landmarks to Riley.

That evening the three natives joined them for supper and Riley gave them some salt pork and Johnny cakes to take with them. They seemed delighted with the gifts and Riley was pleased with their new alliance.

"We couldn't hope for anythin' better," said Riley after they'd gone. "None of them will track for the red-coats, an' they'll tell us where they are."

Paddy looked doubtful. "How do yer know they won't change their minds? I don't trust them."

"I see no reason to distrust them," put in Aaron. "After all, they didn't have to help us. They offered."

Mick nodded in agreement. "I think they hate the settlers as much as we do."

"Aye," said Lawrie. "They took their land, didn't they? Maybe they see us as a way of getting it back."

"That's a bloody long shot," said Paddy with a raised sceptical brow. "More like they'll lead the bloody red-coats straight ter us. They know where we're hiding now."

"Twill be awright," said Riley stretching. "I'm sure of it."

~

Chapter Twelve

Sydney Gaol, August 1825

Tom groaned and tried to roll himself up in the thin blanket. The cold morning air was seeping into his bones and no matter what he couldn't get warm. He opened one eye and looked at John who was sleeping on the narrow crib opposite him. How he could sleep when it was so cold he didn't know. He sighed and wriggled his legs in an attempt to get the blood flowing down to his freezing toes. God, he couldn't feel them anymore.

Following their capture, they'd been sent by boat down to Sydney. He'd expected them to be dragged before the Chief Justice and sentenced to God only knew what horrible punishment, but that hadn't happened. They'd been in prison now for about two weeks and everyday Tom expected them to be sent to trial. He didn't want to think about what they might do to them though. At the very least they'd be sent to some penal settlement like the Newcastle coal mines, or they might decide to hang them. He swallowed and pushed all thoughts of punishment from his mind. It didn't do him any good to dwell on these things.

He rolled over and tried to forget about the cold and what might happen. At least the others had got away and were still obviously on the loose. He hoped they'd burnt Reid's house down as they'd planned. He'd love to know, and he'd have liked to have been there.

It was mid-afternoon by his estimation when Private Barker came to their cell. This was it, he'd come to take them to Court for trial. His stomach clenched and he locked eyes with John briefly. He could see his own trepidation mirrored in John's green eyes.

"Ye have a visitor," said Private Barker unlocking the cell door and standing aside to let the man in.

Tom and John both looked up; surprised. They weren't expecting anyone to visit them. Tom didn't even know anyone who would know where he was. A tall dark haired soldier entered the cell holding his hat under his arm.

"Thank you Private. Give me say twenty minutes."

"Aye sir," he replied.

As soon as the Private had gone down the corridor he turned to the two prisoners.

"Perhaps you remember me. Lieutenant William Hicks," he said introducing himself. "Although, you may remember my wife Sophia better. She cooked you supper one evening."

Tom stared at him. Aye, he remembered raiding Hicks house and his wife cooking them supper. Although he was quite drunk by the time they'd left. He swallowed. What the hell did he want? He looked at John, who shrugged. He hadn't been involved in that particular burglary.

"Aye," Tom finally said. He looked warily at the Lieutenant. Was he going to give evidence against him at trial? Is that why he was here? He licked his lips. "I remember well enough."

"Good, then you'll remember you stole several valuable items from me," said the Lieutenant relaxing somewhat. "In particular, a sapphire brooch belonging to my wife. It was given to her by her mother and she would very much like it back."

"Oh," replied Tom heaving a sigh. So he wasn't here for trial; that was a relief. He didn't particularly remember the brooch the Lieutenant wanted though. Even if he did, they'd traded it for information. It was gone. "Well we don't have it anymore, we would've traded it."

Lieutenant Hicks took in a deep breath and went on undaunted. "Who did you trade it with?"

Tom stared at him, trying to make up his mind whether to tell him or not. He might put in a good word for him if he helped him get the brooch back. He'd have to name names though, and he wasn't sure he wanted to do that. He licked his lips as he thought about it. Maybe it would be worth telling the Lieutenant what he knew. Would it really make any difference to the others?

"I could make it worth your while," said Lieutenant Hicks seeing the conflict on his face. "You do know you'll likely hang for your crimes. I could speak to the Chief

Justice on your behalf if you co-operate with me."

"Don't trust him," said John glaring at Hicks. "He says that now, but yer can't trust him. He's a red-coat."

Tom sucked in a deep breath. That was true enough. You could never trust a red-coat; but what did he have to lose? Perhaps Hicks could influence the sentence – could put in a good word so they wouldn't hang him. Shit, he didn't know what to do. He licked his lips and looked nervously around the small cell, almost hoping to see the answer written on the walls or something.

"What about John?" he said at last. "Ye'd have ter put in a good word for him as well."

Lieutenant Hicks glanced briefly at John before turning his attention back to Tom. "If I recover the brooch, then I'll speak for both of you. But I'll need names."

Tom swallowed and pressed his lips together.

"Don't do it," said John eyeing Hicks. "Yer can't trust him."

"Aye, but what do we have ter lose?" said Tom. "They've already got us, an' it'll make no difference ter the others."

John shrugged. "I wasn't there. Tell him if yer want ter, but I don't trust him ter speak for us."

"You have my word," said Hicks.

Tom looked from one to the other. He took in a deep breath and decided to hope for the best. "Alright I'll tell ye what I know," he said breathing heavily. "I don't remember who we traded the brooch with, but I can give ye several names of people that might have it."

Lieutenant Hicks nodded. "Alright. Who?"

"I remember Richard Martin gave us information in exchange for some baubles," said Tom trying hard to remember the names of some of the settlers they'd visited. There had been so many. At least a dozen or more had sheltered them and given them information. "Also, a Thomas Boardman. They both have small holdings in Wallis Plains."

"Boardman and Martin," said Lieutenant Hicks committing the names to memory. "Anyone else?"

"Oh, aye there's another one that might have ye brooch," said Tom scratching his head. "I think his name was Jones. William Jones."

"I hope you're not sending me on a wild goose chase?" said Hicks eyeing him.

"No, I swear."

"If I'm successful in recovering my property then you have my word I'll speak with the Chief Justice concerning your case," he said putting on his hat. "Good day."

"Wait," said Tom jumping to his feet.

Hicks turned and raised his eyebrows.

"Did they burn Reid's house?"

The Lieutenant looked down his rather long nose at Tom, a look of disgust on his face. "They did."

He opened the cell door and called to Private Barker who came running down the corridor.

"Yes sir."

193

Without a word or a backward look, he marched down the hall leaving the Private to close the cell door. Tom sat down and sighed. He hoped to God he'd done the right thing. It was too late now if he hadn't.

~

Lieutenant Hicks was furious as he left the barracks. He shouldn't have told them about Reid's homestead, but he'd been caught off guard. He begrudgingly admitted he hadn't expected them to be quite so co-operative. Still, he consoled himself with the fact that he had names. Names of settlers who had helped the buggers.

He wondered if he should take that information straight to Alexander Scott and have them arrested. He sidestepped a pile of manure as he made his way down to the docks. No, he wouldn't get Sophia's brooch back if he did that. He was better off approaching these men himself. He'd threaten them if had to, and then he might have them arrested as well.

That afternoon he boarded the cutter Elizabeth Henrietta bound for Newcastle.

He was anxious to be home, not that he'd be seeing Sophia and his baby son. They'd be staying in Sydney until this whole bushranging affair was over. Sophia had been so traumatised by them that she was too afraid to stay with him in Wallis Plains. He hoped it wouldn't be too long before they were brought to justice.

The Elizabeth Henrietta docked in Newcastle early the following morning and William disembarked as soon as he could. He was anxious to get to Wallis Plains as quickly as possible. He could either take one of the boats that plied the river or buy a horse and take the bridle path. It would certainly be more comfortable by boat, but it would take longer. He sighed. He didn't have enough money to purchase a horse, even if he could find one for sale. No, he'd have to take the riverboat.

The day was cool and overcast but for the moment it was dry. He cast his eyes skyward. The clouds looked dark and heavy with rain; it would no doubt pour before midday. He hurried along the wharf to where the riverboats came in. He let out the breath he'd been holding. One of the small river crafts was tied up at the wharf. They were generally only in port once or twice a week, and he couldn't believe his luck.

He paid the passage to Wallis Plains and boarded the small vessel. It mainly carried freight up the river, and occasionally it would bring convicts and other passengers downriver. Today it was transporting a pig and two bullocks as well as Government provisions for the small settlement of Patrick Plains. William would be sharing a very small and cramped cabin with a Mr George Peters. He was a portly middle-aged man with a frightful case of bad breath.

He immediately set to telling him all about the difficulty he was having in obtaining a land grant. "I believe the Acting Governor is too afraid to make a damn decision," he said. "You'd think he'd be delighted to have someone of my calibre wanting to take up land. But no." He paused to take a breath before droning on further about the lack of foresight.

William took the opportunity to excuse himself, feigning the need for some fresh air. He stepped out onto the deck of the boat and took several deep breaths. The air smelled of rotting fish, but it was better than being in the company of Mr Peters. He stayed up on deck until the inclement weather drove him inside. He was anxious to be underway, but the Captain informed him they would need the incoming tide to navigate the river. He sighed and tried to relax, and ignore his fellow passengers.

The trip up river to Wallis Plains would take about twelve hours and two tides. They cast off on the evening tide and following a simple supper of fish and rice William took himself off to bed. He spent a restless night tossing and turning on the narrow bunk, and wasn't feeling any more rested in the morning than he had the night before. He was in a foul mood by the time he disembarked at the small pier at Wallis Plains.

Not being familiar with any of the men whom he was looking for, he headed for the barracks. He thought the constable, John Allen, or some of the soldiers stationed there might know where he could find them. He shivered as he made his away along the muddy road to the barracks. It was a cold morning with a slight drizzle of rain.

He arrived in no time, opened the door and stepped inside. There was a small fire burning in the grate and he immediately headed for it. He rubbed his cold hands in front of it until he finally got some warmth into his fingers.

"Lieutenant Hicks," said John Allen smiling at him from across the room. "This is a pleasant surprise. I trust ye are well."

"Aye, I am thank you," replied William.

"I trust you know Private McCain?" he said gesturing to the young soldier who moments ago had been lounging in one of the chairs.

"I do," said William nodding to the young Private before turning his attention back to the constable. "I wonder if I could prevail upon you for some information."

"Of course. How can we be of assistance?"

"I'm looking for three men. A Richard Martin, Thomas Boardman and William Jones," he said. "I believe the first two may have small holdings, of Jones I have no idea."

"Aye. I believe William Jones has a few acres north of town, on the right hand side. Thomas Boardman has a house here in town down by the river, not far from the bridge. It's the last one before you get to the river."

"Thank you," said William smiling. He couldn't have hoped for better information. "What about Martin? Any ideas at all?"

John Allen shook his head. "No, I don't know him. What about you Henry, have you heard of a Richard Martin?"

Private McCain looked into space for a moment. "I don't know 'bout a Richard Martin, but ol' Tom Martin's got a house down by the Wallis Creek. He might know him."

"Thank you. You've both been most helpful," said William putting on his hat and taking his leave of them. He couldn't wait to track the men down.

~

Chapter Thirteen

Wallis Plains

The weather turned wet and squally and the five men spent the next week confined to their hut. They had enough supplies to last them a few more days, but they'd definitely need to get fresh provisions soon. The three natives had returned several nights ago and spent the evening with them. They were still on friendly terms with them, although Aaron wondered how long that would last.

Riley had promised them they'd burn as many fields of wheat as they could. They had smiled and nodded and Birrani promised they'd help them do it when the time came. He hoped Riley knew what he was doing. He suspected the natives would quickly lose interest if they didn't burn more of the settlers' homes down.

However, he was more anxious to find out what the others planned to do. Eventually, they would get caught unless they got away, not just from Wallis Plains, but from New South Wales.

"We ought to head for the coast and get ourselves on a ship," he suggested one night while they were sitting around the fire. "The only way we'll ever be truly free is we get away from here."

Riley nodded but was noncommittal.

"Aye I think yer right," said Lawrie spitting a wad of tobacco. "We should get enough provisions together an' head for the coast."

"Where would we go?" said Mick frowning.

"America," said Paddy looking excited. "Ain't no red-coats there."

"Yer talkin' piracy," said Riley, at last, joining the conversation. "How else do yer expect ter git on a ship?"

"We could stowaway," said Mick running his fingers through his greying hair. "Or we could pay passage maybe."

"I don't fancy stealing a ship," said Aaron shaking his head. "None of us know anything about sailing. We wouldn't even make it out of the harbour."

They all nodded and murmured agreement with Aaron. He was right; they'd have no hope of stealing a ship and sailing it to America.

"I reckon our best bet would be ter pretend ter be respectable merchants an' pay our fares," said Lawrie. "We could steal enough money an' the right kind of clothes - I reckon we'd get away with it."

"Aye, I reckon we would," put in Paddy. "Twould be easy enough ter steal some decent clothes."

The conversation went around in circles for another hour or so, and no agreement was made. Aaron sighed. If he wanted to leave he'd have to go it alone. He actually thought he'd have more chance of success by himself. Perhaps he should ask one of the natives to be his guide and take him to the coast. He didn't like the idea of leaving his mates behind, but they didn't appear to have any thoughts for the future.

They spent the next day preparing to raid for fresh supplies. They cleaned their firearms and Paddy made a fresh batch of Johnny cakes for the journey. It was late afternoon when they set off along the well-worn track along the creek towards Wallis Plains. The weather had improved somewhat. The rain had eased and there were patches of blue sky visible between the clouds. Aaron thought they'd likely get a frost tonight as a result.

They skirted around the small hamlet of Wallis Plains and continued on the southern side of the river. There were a few smaller properties on the township side of the river. They bypassed several smaller farms and crossed a narrow creek lined with river gums and climbed the bank on the other side. Up ahead Aaron could see the dark outline of a farmhouse set among some large acacia trees. The yard at the front had been cleared and it had a wide veranda along the front. He thought the trees would provide plenty of cool shade in the summer.

Riley pulled his pistol out of his belt. "Someone's home. There's smoke comin' outta the chimney."

"I hope they've got some fresh meat," said Paddy grinning at him. "I fancy a bit of beef."

Lawrie chuckled. "Aye with peas an' potatoes," he said taking hold of his musket with both hands, his finger ready on the trigger.

Aaron and Mick likewise readied their firearms. They were halfway across the yard when two windows at the front of the house opened. Without a word of warning three shots rang out. They'd obviously seen them coming and opened fire.

"Aargh," screamed Lawrie putting his hand to his shoulder. Blood began oozing in between his fingers causing a dark stain to spread outward on his waistcoat. "Shit!"

Aaron thought he heard three distinct shots and he dived for the ground. His heart was hammering as he got to his knees, and took aim and fired his musket.

Riley and Paddy returned fire as well before grabbing Lawrie and hauling him back to the relative cover of some nearby bushes. Mick fired at them and then ran for it as well.

Aaron scrambled to his feet and joined them behind the bushes. The men in the house reloaded and fired another round in their direction.

"I reckon I hit one of 'em," came a man's excited voice from the house.

"Get off my land," yelled another.

Riley was undaunted and reloaded his pistol and fired again. Aaron likewise reloaded his musket but thought he was too far away to hit his mark. Paddy and Mick fired again, but their shots fell short.

Lawrie was sitting down leaning up against the trunk of a small wattle tree. He looked as white as a sheet as he tried to stem the bleeding from his shoulder. Aaron put his musket down and went to assist him. His waistcoat was soaked with blood and he helped him first remove his jacket and then he shrugged out of the waistcoat. There was a neat hole in his shirt where the shot had gone in, just below his collar bone. Blood was soaking into the cotton shirt turning it russet red. Aaron pulled the shirt collar loose to look at the wound. It was a small neat hole which was oozing blood.

He took a handkerchief out of his pocket and folded it neatly before pressing it onto the wound. He peered at Lawrie, who looked like he was about to pass out. His face was covered in a sheen of sweat, but he shivered.

"You'll be alright," said Aaron taking off his jacket and putting over Lawrie. "Press on the wound to stop the bleeding."

Another round of muskets was fired from the house, and Aaron felt a ball go whizzing close to his ear. He ducked down and looked towards the house. Three muzzles were visible jutting out of the windows pointed in their direction. He sucked in a large breath and picked up his musket.

"We ain't gonna git anywhere near them," said Riley panting. "We'll have ter try elsewhere."

"Aye," said Aaron. He was glad Riley had conceded it was a lost cause. "We need to get Lawrie some help. He's losing a lot of blood."

Riley glanced at him. He looked pale and sweaty and was sitting by the tree with his eyes closed. "Aye. Let's git outta here."

Paddy got on one side of Lawrie and Mick on the other and they hauled him to his feet. He groaned horribly, but at least he didn't pass out. They half carried, half dragged him away from the house. Aaron picked up Lawrie's discarded musket and followed them.

"Any idea where we can take him?" said Aaron glancing nervously behind them. He hoped they wouldn't be pursued, but he had his musket ready just in case.

"Aye," said Paddy panting as they crossed the creek. "We ought ter take him ter Tom Boardman, he's a surgeon."

"He's a horse surgeon," said Riley raising his eyebrows. Lawrie's head was lolling to one side and he looked pale. Riley wasn't sure if he'd passed out or not. "Aye, twould be better than no one, an' we can't take him to a regular surgeon."

Mick paused to get a better grip on Lawrie. "He might call the constable," he said alarm clear in his voice.

"No he won't," said Paddy groaning under Lawrie's weight. "He's helped us afore. We've traded stuff with him for information an' such."

"Aye," said Riley taking Paddy's place, and grabbing Lawrie firmly under his arm. "He doesn't live far from here. Down by the river near the bridge."

"Let's go," said Paddy taking the lead as they made their way back towards Wallis Plains.

It was dark by the time they arrived at Tom Boardman's back door. Aaron glanced around the yard nervously. They were awfully close to town and the likelihood of being seen by neighbours and the like was making him wary. Riley knocked on the door and waited.

A minute later the door opened a crack and a large man with a mop of mousy coloured hair peered out at them. Recognition dawned on his face immediately and he opened the door a little wider. He glanced around at them and his yard before he stepped aside to allow them to enter.

"I wasn't expectin' ye," he said eyeing them as they stepped into his kitchen. He immediately noticed Lawrie who was half carried inside by Mick and Aaron. They put him down in a wooden chair by the hearth. "What happened to him?"

A middle-aged woman came into the kitchen. Her greying hair was pulled up into a bun and her bright blue eyes glowed with friendly warmth. "Good evenin'," she said smiling at them.

"My wife Mary," said Tom Boardman.

"Evenin' Ma'am. I believe we've met afore," said Riley smiling warmly at her before turning his attention back to Tom. "Lawrie here's been shot, an' we were hopin' yer might be able ter help him."

"I'll make us some tea shall I?" said Mary Boardman, and without waiting for a response set about putting the water on to boil.

William scratched his head and stared at Riley. "Ye do know I'm not that sort of surgeon don't ye?"

"Aye," put in Paddy. "But we can't be takin' him ter a regular surgeon now can we?"

"He's got a musket ball in his shoulder," said Riley. "We can make it worth yer while. We'll have some goods ter trade in a day or so."

Mary turned from her tea preparations to inspect Lawrie. "Not in the parlour Tom. Lay him out on the table here."

Tom eyed his wife and sighed. "Alright, I'll see what I can do."

Riley and Paddy with Aaron's help lifted Lawrie onto the wooden table and laid him out. He was awake and he groaned and grunted when they moved him. Aaron thought it'd be better if he'd passed out. It was going to hurt like hell getting that shot out of his shoulder. He grimaced and stepped away from the table.

Tom undid Lawrie's shirt and peeled it away from his shoulder. He removed the handkerchief that Aaron had placed over the wound. It was stuck to his skin with dried blood and Lawrie yelped when William tore it away. He peered at the wound and prodded it with his large meaty fingers. Lawrie let out a low moan in response.

"Fetch the brandy Mary," he said to his wife. "I'll go get the pincers an' see if we can get this ball out."

Aaron swallowed. He was bloody glad it wasn't him that was about to be prodded and poked with a pair of pincers. He stepped as far away from the table as he could. He took a Johnnycake out of his pocket and began munching. He was hungry and it didn't look like he'd be getting supper anytime soon.

Mary returned a few minutes later with a decanter of brandy which she placed on the table for her husband. She then prepared the tea and poured a mug for each of them. Aaron thanked her and nervously gulped down some of the sweet black substance. It was good and it helped him to relax.

Tom returned with a pair of pincers, a knife and some strips of material. Aaron assumed he'd be using the latter to bind Lawrie's shoulder once the ball had been removed. He also had a small strip of leather with him, probably from an old bridle or something.

"Bite down hard on this," he said putting it between Lawrie's teeth. "Are ye ready?"

Lawrie was pale and looked terrified, but he nodded.

"Alright. I want ye lads to hold him still. Hold his legs an' arms as best ye can."

Riley grabbed hold of his uninjured right shoulder and Paddy held on to his left arm. Mick and Aaron took hold of a leg each. Aaron was glad he was as far away from the operation as he could be. He swallowed and pressed his lips together. Shit, he'd be glad when this was over. He could only imagine how Lawrie was feeling.

"Alright then. Hold him still," said Tom taking the brandy and pouring some liberally on the wound.

Aaron winced as Lawrie let out a stifled yell. He swallowed and breathed in heavily through his nose. God, he was glad it wasn't him. He turned away as Tom took the pincers in hand and began prodding the wound for the ball. Lawrie went even paler as he began panting through his nose. His yells were stifled by the leather strip in his mouth, but it was obvious he was in agony.

Lawrie was squirming and screaming, but they all hung onto him and kept him as still as they could. Aaron could feel his flesh quivering under his fingers. He kept his eyes averted. He didn't want to see what was happening. Lawrie's cries were enough to chill him to the bone, he didn't need to see.

After a bit, Lawrie quieted and Aaron took a look at him. Thank God, the poor bastard had passed out. Tom continued to prod the wound for the ball, and after a few minutes withdrew the pincers with a flattened piece of lead held firmly between them. He dropped it into the palm of his hand and inspected it.

"What was he wearin'," he asked as he peeled a layer of cloth away from the piece of lead.

"What?" said Riley clearly confused by the question.

"How many layers of clothin'?" he said turning to Riley. "The ball's passed through several layers I'd say. I need to know how many."

"Oh," realisation dawning on him. "A shirt an' a jacket," he said looking around the small kitchen. Lawrie's discarded jacket was hanging on the back of a chair.

"And a waistcoat," put in Aaron. "It was blood soaked so I took it off him."

"Ah," said Tom looking closely at the piece of lead in his hand. He rubbed it between his fingers and another piece of fabric separated from it. "Well, it looks like there's still one piece in there."

Aaron swallowed. How the hell was he going to get that out?

Tom handed the lead and pieces of cloth to his wife and proceeded to prod the wound further. Aaron grimaced as blood oozed down Lawrie's shoulder. Minutes ticked by and still, Tom was prodding around in Lawrie's shoulder. Aaron knew that if he didn't get it out the wound would fester, and would no doubt prove fatal. It still might, but he'd have a better chance if they got it out.

Finally, Tom withdrew the pincers, with a small fragment of cloth tightly clutched between its jaws. Aaron heaved a massive sigh of relief, as did Tom. He put the pincers aside and poured more brandy into the wound before winding several layers of bandages around Lawrie's shoulder.

"Well I've done the best I can," he said. "I can't say if he'll recover or no."

"Thank yer," said Riley clearly as relieved that it was over. "I wonder if we could prevail on yer for one more thing?"

"Aye," said Tom warily.

"Could yer keep him for the night? We'll come by in the mornin' for him."

Tom looked at his patient lying on his kitchen table. He was quite unconscious and it would be difficult to move him. He looked at Mary, who nodded.

He groaned. "Alright, but he can't stay here. Help me get him into the back room."

"Thank yer," smiled Riley. "Come on lads, git a hold of him. Lead the way, Tom."

They carried the comatose Lawrie into a small back room off the kitchen which had a narrow bed in one corner. The rest of the room was taken up with crates and boxes. They put him down on the bed and Mary Boardman covered him with a quilt.

"Ye needn't worry about him, he'll be just fine here until mornin'," said Mary smiling at them.

"Thank yer," said Riley. "We'll see yer in the mornin' then. Come on lads we best git outta here."

Aaron had no idea what time it was as they left the Boardman's house. It was cold and frosty and he imagined it was probably somewhere near midnight. They made their way back to their hut without any further incidents and went straight to bed. Aaron yawned widely as he wrapped himself in his blanket. He hoped to God Lawrie would be alright. Then he smiled to himself. He hadn't actually thought about God for quite some time. Perhaps a prayer wouldn't go amiss.

~

Chapter Fourteen

The Boardman's Residence

Lieutenant Hicks was feeling quite disheartened as he made his way down the road towards the river. He'd turned up empty handed the previous day at Martin's place. Old Tom Martin was completely deaf and even though he'd yelled loudly at him, it had been hopeless. He didn't read either, and so trying to write down who he was looking for hadn't helped. The visit had been a complete and utter waste of his time.

He'd had better luck with William Jones. He'd had some difficulty finding the house as John Allen's description of it had been rather vague. In fact, he'd spent the best part of yesterday trying to find the damned place.

As it turned out, he had a number of cleared acres on which he was running sheep, and quite a sizeable farmhouse. However, he didn't have Sophia's brooch. Of that he was confident. He'd threatened to have the man arrested, and he'd pretty quickly come up with quite a stash of stolen goods. The Jacob's mob had traded the baubles with him for information and shelter. Hicks planned to deliver the items to Don McLeod as soon as he had time. He was sure he'd get the items back to their rightful owners.

However, Sophia's brooch hadn't been amongst them. He'd run out of time to track down Thomas Boardman yesterday, and so this morning he planned on visiting him first thing. If he had no luck there, well he'd have to ask around about the elusive Richard Martin.

It was a chilly morning, but there were patches of blue sky and a weak wintry sun was peeking out between the clouds. He arrived at the end of the main road where it crossed the river. He paused and looked about. John Allen had said Boardman lived near the bridge down by the river. He noticed a narrow muddy road heading east from the bridge and through the trees he thought he could see a house.

He urged his horse down the road, and after going a short way found the house.

It was a single story timber house perched high on the river bank. It had a well kept front garden and what looked like some sizeable outbuildings. He dismounted and tied his horse to the front fence. He stretched before walking up the path to the front door. He admired the garden as went, and couldn't help thinking that Sophia would like one just like this. He quickly brought his thoughts back to the matter at hand as he got to the end of the path. He took in a deep breath and knocked loudly on the door.

It was opened not more than a minute later, although William suspected that the inhabitants had first peeped out the window at him. He'd seen the curtains move. He sighed.

"Can I help ye?" asked a grey-haired woman who smiled warmly at him.

"Aye. I'm Lieutenant William Hicks, and I'm looking for Thomas Boardman. Have I got the right house?"

"Oh aye, but ye'll need to take ye horse around back."

"Oh no," he said smiling at her. "I'm not here about my horse. May I come in?"

She cast him an odd look and quickly looked over her shoulder. "Of course Lieutenant. Please make ye self comfortable in the parlour, an' I'll fetch me, husband," she said stepping aside for him to enter.

He removed his hat and entered the house, which opened straight into a small shabby parlour. "Thank you," he said looking around the room. There was a threadbare sofa against one wall and two armchairs with grubby looking rugs tossed over them. He decided to stand and wait for Thomas Boardman to appear.

Mrs Boardman hurried from the room calling to her husband as she went. "Tom there's a Lieutenant here to see ye."

A few minutes later a large mousy haired man arrived in the parlour. All of a sudden the room seemed even smaller and William took a step back.

"Mr Boardman? Thomas Boardman?"

"Aye I am," he replied eyeing William warily.

William puffed out his chest and stared Boardman in the eye. "I have it on good authority that you've been harbouring bushrangers, and accepting their ill gotten gain."

Shock and surprise registered momentarily on Tom Boardman face as he stared at William. However, he recovered himself quickly. "What makes ye think such a thing?"

"Two of the bushrangers are in custody in Sydney, and they told me of your activities."

Tom licked his lips and looked nervously about. "What do ye want Lieutenant?"

A satisfied look went over William's face. He didn't want to beat about the bush and was glad that Boardman had been so quick on the uptake. "I simply wish to recover some property belonging to my wife. A sapphire brooch. Have you seen such a thing?"

Tom Boardman nodded. "Is that all ye want?"

William eyed him for a moment and sucked in a deep breath. He really only wanted to recover the brooch, but if

Boardman had more perhaps he should take it. Tom saw the uncertainty in his eyes.

"Mary," he called to his wife. She appeared moments later.

"Aye."

"Fetch the sapphire brooch for the Lieutenant."

"What?" she said surprised at her husband's request. Her blue eyes locked briefly with his and a look passed between them. She nodded before disappearing through the nearest door.

She returned a minute later with the brooch in hand, and without a word handed it to Lieutenant Hicks. He looked at it before smiling and putting it safely in his pocket. Sophia would be so delighted he'd recovered it. He could hardly wait to write to her with the good news.

"Thank you. My wife will be most appreciative to have this returned to her."

"Well if there's naught else we can do for ye, I have a busy day ahead," said Tom clearly anxious to see the back of the Lieutenant. "And I trust we'll not hear anymore about this?"

William considered them for a moment, before putting on his hat and opening the door. "You need not fear Mr Boardman. However, if I hear of you harbouring the outlaws in the future I will not be so lenient. Good day."

Without another word, he stepped outside shutting the door firmly behind him. He took in a deep breath and went down the path to the road. He mounted his horse and turned towards Wallis Plains. He cast a glance back at the house before he set off down the road. He could've sworn Mrs Boardman was watching him from the window. How very odd.

~

"He's gone," called Mary Boardman letting the curtain go and hurrying out to the kitchen.

Aaron breathed a sigh of relief. That had been way too close for comfort. They'd arrived to collect Lawrie not long before Hicks had knocked on the door, and had remained quiet in the kitchen for the duration of his visit. Aaron didn't think Tom would've been so quick to hand over the brooch otherwise.

"We're sorry yer had ter give it back on our account," said Riley to Mary when she came back into the kitchen.

She smiled weakly at him. "Tis alright."

Tom put his arm around his wife and sighed. "We can't help ye again, an' don't bring us anythin' in payment. We cannot risk the Lieutenant findin' out."

Riley nodded.

"I'm sorry ter bring trouble ter yer door," said Lawrie earnestly. "I canna thank yer enough for yer help." He shrugged into his jacket leaving the left sleeve hanging limp. His left arm was in a makeshift sling as Tom had suggested.

"Ye welcome," said Tom. "I hope ye mend well enough."

"So do I," said Lawrie grimacing. "Tis stiff an' sore this morning I can tell yer, an' I've got a dull ache in my bones."

Tom nodded. "I expect twill be sore until it heals," he said opening the back door and peering out. The yard was empty and he gestured to them to leave.

They filed out of the house and into the cool morning air. Lawrie was still very pale and he appeared to Aaron to be in a fair amount of pain. Still, he didn't complain as they made their way back to the hut. Lawrie would be spending at least the next few days resting and recovering from his ordeal. The others however still needed to get fresh supplies.

"I still have a hankering fer some fresh beef," said Paddy.

"There ain't no guarantee that whoever we rob will have some," said Mick.

"Mick's right," put in Riley. "There's only one way ter be sure of gittin' fresh beef, an' that's killin' it ourselves."

Aaron nodded and wondered if Riley was serious. He had no idea about butchering an animal, however, he thought Paddy and Riley would. They'd both been farmers back in Ireland.

Paddy grinned. "So all we've got ter do is find ourselves a nice fat bullock."

"Aye an' yer can cook us a nice roast beef," said Riley licking his lips at the prospect.

"I don't know nothin' about killin' a bullock," put in Mick looking worried. "I know about horses, not cattle."

"Nor do I," said Aaron.

"Don't worry. Paddy an' me know what ter do," said Riley grinning at them. "Besides, ain't nothin' ter it really. If yer can swing an axe yer can butcher a bullock."

Aaron was glad to hear that Riley and Paddy knew what they were doing because he was with Mick when it came to butchering. "Do you reckon the natives would like in on it?" he said. He thought they would.

"Aye probably," said Paddy. "But we're not goin' ter wait for them are we?"

"No tellin' when they'll come by again," said Riley rubbing his chin. "We'll share it with 'em, but we're not waitin' for 'em."

~

It was just after midday when the four of them set off to find a bullock. Lawrie was in no shape to join them, so he stayed behind at the hut. They equipped

226

themselves with firearms, sharp knives and an axe as well as a supply of water and several hessian bags. They would have to butcher the animal where they killed it and carry what meat they could back with them.

They headed west following the Wallis Creek which flowed through a large property belonging to George Rutherford. They continued along the creek until it joined the Hunter River east of another large farm run by Standish Harris. There was a wire fence separating the two properties which went all the way down to the river. They climbed over it and continued on. They were meandering through a grove of wattle trees when Paddy spotted a good size bullock grazing on some tussocks. He stopped and pointed to the animal.

Aaron peered through the trees until finally, he spotted it. He glanced around. The animal appeared to be alone and unaware of their presence. He waited nervously while Riley and Paddy crept through the trees towards it.

They kept a good fifteen feet or so from the animal while they circled around behind it. Riley got himself into position in front of the animal, his musket at the ready. Paddy waved his arms in the air to get its attention. As soon as it put its head up Riley fired, shooting it right between the eyes. It bellowed and dropped to the ground immediately, although Aaron didn't think it was dead. Paddy shot it again to be sure.

By the time Aaron and Mick made their way to where the animal was lying Riley had taken his knife and cut its throat. Blood was gushing everywhere. Aaron glanced nervously about. He hoped the shots hadn't been heard or else they could expect company soon. All he could hear was the sound of a few crows calling in the distance; no voices or sounds of people coming.

"Is it dead?" he asked holding the axe out to Riley.

"Aye. I don't need that yet. We'll need ter gut it first," said Riley grinning at him.

"Give me hand ter roll it over," said Paddy groaning as he tried to move the beast.

Between the four of them, they got the animal on its back and Paddy took his knife and proceeded to slit it open from its sternum to its anus. He then peeled back the skin and muscle and sliced out the liver and other innards.

Aaron had been holding his breath, expecting the odour to be putrid. He was surprised when he finally took a breath to find it was just a strong animal smell. An earthy humid odour seemed to permeate over the top of that, but it wasn't anywhere near as disgusting as he'd imagined it would be.

Riley cut around the hoofs and sliced down the inside of each leg and began separating the hide from the animal. It appeared to Aaron that the hide just peeled off as he deftly flicked his knife under the skin. Once the skin had been peeled back along the sides of the animal they let it go and rolled it back onto its side.

"We won't be able ter skin the whole thing," said Riley putting his knife in his belt. "We'd need ter hang it ter do that, an' ain't no way the four of us could lift it."

"No the bloody thing must weigh a ton," said Paddy getting to his feet. He was covered in blood and guts, but he didn't appear to care. "Give me the axe."

Aaron handed him the axe and stood back while Paddy proceeded to butcher the animal. Riley was making suggestions as to where he should make the cuts. Flesh and blood flew off the end of the axe as Paddy struck the beast. Aaron swallowed. This was by far the most gruesome part of the whole procedure as far as he was concerned. He grimaced as he was sprayed with blood and bits of fat and meat.

As each chunk of meat was separated from the bullock Riley tossed it to Mick and Aaron to put in one of the bags they'd brought with them. Riley and Paddy worked away, taking it in turns with the axe until they'd filled their bags with as much as they could carry. It was late in the afternoon before they finished, and hoicking the bags over their shoulders headed back to their hut.

"It'll be ter late ter roast a piece of this tonight, but we could cut some steaks," said Riley climbing over the fence as they headed back along the creek.

"Aye, I canna remember the last time I had steak," said Mick licking his lips at the thought.

"Steaks it is then," said Paddy grinning. "We might even have a few peas we can have with that."

Aaron sighed. Fresh meat whichever way it was cooked was going to be a real treat.

~

Chapter Fifteen

The Hut, early September 1825

Mick and Paddy went out scouting the next day for a likely farmhouse to raid for supplies. They had plenty of fresh meat but it wouldn't keep long. They needed other supplies like tea, flour and salt pork. They arrived back around mid-afternoon with news that Vicars Jacob had appointed a new overseer.

"Do we know him?" asked Riley.

"No I don't think so," replied Paddy stoking the fire. "We ran into Rob Morley an' he said he came up from Sydney. Said his name's Richard Hines."

Riley nodded. "How's Rob? Does he wanna join us?"

Paddy shook his head and shrugged. "He didna say."

Lawrie let out a moan from the corner of the room where he was lying wrapped in a blanket.

"Is he awright?" asked Mick his brow creasing in concern.

"I think he's got a fever," said Aarons shaking his head. "When I felt his forehead earlier it was hot and clammy."

"Shit," said Riley peering at him. "Twas always a risk that could happen."

"Is there anythin' we can do?" asked Mick.

Riley shrugged. "I dunno."

"Anyways, I think we ought ter pay the new overseer a visit," said Paddy grinning at them.

"Oh aye I agree with yer," replied Riley a wide smile spreading across his face. "Twould be the polite thing ter do. We'll go tonight."

"Awright," agreed Paddy smiling happily. "In the meantime, I'll get some of that bullock on ter roast fer supper."

In no time at all the smell of roasting meat filled the hut. Paddy had a huge piece of beef on the grill which he was periodically turning over the hot coals. Aaron breathed in the heavenly smell and his stomach grumbled. He couldn't wait til supper time.

It was just on dusk when they heard noises outside the hut. Riley opened the door cautiously. "Oh hello," he greeted their visitors. "Tis Birrani, Yarran an' Ngarra," he said turning to tell the others. "Come in."

The three natives entered the small cramped hut, which was now full to bursting. They were wearing their usual possum cloaks and face paint, although Aaron noticed they'd left their spears outside.

"Yer must stay fer supper," said Paddy gesturing to his roasting meat on the fire. "We've plenty fer everyone."

"Aye thank ye," said Birrani smelling the air. "Li-yandharra," he said *we eat together* to Yarran and Ngarra, and they nodded and smiled.

Birrani noticed Lawrie lying on the floor in the corner and raised a questioning brow pointing to him.

"He's sick," said Riley. Birrani continued to look questioning at him. "He was shot. Yer know he's hurt." Riley picked up the nearest musket and pointed it at Lawrie. "Bang."

Realisation dawned on Birrani's broad face and he nodded. He knelt beside Lawrie and ran his bony fingers over his forehead and face. Lawrie moaned but otherwise didn't protest.

"Nhila mambuwar. Yarran dugayilinya ngangkari Killara," he said getting to his feet and addressing Yarran. *He's unwell. Yarran, go and fetch the healer Killara.*

Without a word, Yarran opened the door and left.

Riley, Mick and Aaron looked questioningly at Birrani.

"Yarran gets help," he said noticing their enquiring looks.

"Oh thank yer," smiled Riley.

"I think this beef's ready," said Paddy poking it with a knife and watching the juices run out. He sank a knife into the other end of it and lifted it from the fire and onto the rough kitchen bench. It was a slab of gum tree that had been affixed to the wall next to a wooden trough. He carved a small piece off one the end and popped it into his mouth.

"Oh it's good," he said grinning at them. He then turned his attention to the large pot hanging over the fire. He lifted the lid and scooped some of the rice and peas onto the end of his knife and tasted them. "They're ready. Let's eat."

Riley carved off slabs of meat for each of them and Paddy dished out the rice and peas. Aaron was ravenous and set to eating his supper with relish. It was delicious, even better than the steaks had been the previous night. He wished there'd been some gravy to go with it, but he wasn't about to complain. He noticed that Birrani and Ngarra were not eating with as much gusto as the rest of them. Maybe they hadn't had bullock before. He shrugged, all the more for them if they didn't like it.

They were just finishing their supper when Yarran returned. He had two native women with him. They were also wearing possum cloaks, and one had a woven basket slung over her shoulder which appeared to have a variety of leaves and bark sticking out of it. The older of the two women was wearing several lengths of beads around her neck made of seed pods. Birrani introduced her as Ngangkari Killara. She was the healer. The other younger woman he introduced as Lowanna.

Killara immediately spotted Lawrie lying on the floor and went to look at him. She ran her hands over his face and he moaned when she pulled back his blanket. He was still wearing the bloodied shirt, which she also pushed aside. The bandage around his shoulder was bloody and giving off a sickly sweet odour.

"Mula galing," said Killara turning to Lowanna and gesturing to the fire.

"What does she want?" asked Riley raising a brow at Birrani.

"Water on the fire," said Birrani. "Make hot."

"Oh aye," replied Paddy, and he set about putting a billy of water on to boil. He added another log to the fire and gave the coals a stir, before filling the billy with water from the canteen hanging on a hook by the door.

Killara began unwinding the bandage from Lawrie's shoulder. He was awake but delirious and he groaned and grunted as she worked. The final piece was stuck to his skin with dried blood. Undaunted she wrenched it free. Lawrie winced and sucked in a couple of deep breaths.

Even from the other side of the room, Aaron could see Lawrie's shoulder was red and inflamed. All around the wound was swollen and festering. Killara prodded around the edges of it with her long fingers, all the time muttering in her own strange language. Some discoloured blood oozed from the wound which smelled sweet and unwholesome. Aaron grimaced and turned away.

Lowanna seemed to know exactly what Killara was talking about. She took several of the leaves and a piece of bark from the bag and added it to the billy. As the leaves started to heat they emitted a strange aroma. Aaron thought it smelled a bit like camphor. He was intrigued as to what the women were going to do with it. Was Lawrie supposed to drink it? He had no idea.

The men were all intrigued by the native healers. They had never seen native medicine and it was all rather foreign.

Aaron just hoped it would work. Lawrie's shoulder was obviously festering and he had a high fever.

After a while, Lowanna took the billy off the fire and taking a short piece of wood that looked like a small club from the bag proceeded to pound the leaves and bark. The camphor smell became even stronger and permeated the whole hut. Aaron breathed it in. It wasn't unpleasant exactly just very overpowering.

She set the concoction aside and took several different branches from the bag. These had silvery feathery leaves and she placed one whole branch on the fire. As soon as the leaves started to smoulder Lowanna removed it and began waving the smoking branches over Lawrie. The smoke stung Aaron's eyes and smelled like turpentine. Lawrie coughed and then groaned.

Killara was still talking away in her own language and pressing all around the wound which was now oozing a foul-smelling mix of pus and blood. Aaron grimaced and turned away. He was starting to feel a bit queasy with all the strange smells and the horrible odour coming from Lawrie's shoulder. He noticed Yarran and Ngarra had stepped outside, and he wondered if he should join them.

Lowanna seemed satisfied that the smoke had done its job and she handed the branches to Birrani to take outside. She then took the billy of camphor smelling leaves and bark over to Killara. She nodded and took the concoction from her. She scooped some out and squeezed the liquid from it before applying it to Lawrie's shoulder. It was like a poultice of leaves and bark which she pressed into and around the wound. She pulled the blanket back up over Lawrie and got to her feet.

Aaron took this to mean that she had done all she could. He hoped it would be enough. Only time would tell. He opened the door and went outside. All the strange smells had started to make him feel very odd. He was surprised to see that Yarran and Ngarra were constructing what looked like a temporary shelter beside the hut. It looked large enough for two or three people and was made using several branches covered in bark and bound together. Birrani was lining the inside with soft grevillea branches. He smiled at Aaron.

"Lowanna and Killara will stay," he said in answer to the curious look on Aaron's face.

"Oh aye." He hadn't expected the women to be staying. Of course, he had no idea where they lived or how far away it was. If they were going to care for Lawrie he supposed it only made sense for them to stay close. He breathed the fresh air into his lungs and watched the natives with interest.

For the next four days, the women continued to treat Lawrie with their strange smelling concoctions. Birrani also visited every day. He brought fresh leaves and bark along with yams and other edible plants. Aaron thought the hut was smelling a lot more wholesome than it had. He wondered if some of the plants they'd brought had been for this very purpose.

Lawrie's high fever and delirium broke on the fourth day. By the evening he was even feeling well enough to eat a small bowl of rice and peas. Aaron and the others were equally surprised and pleased with his recovery. Aaron had been sceptical of the

241

native's healing powers. He still wasn't sure if they would be able to stop the wound from festering. He hoped so, but he had his doubts.

It was strange having women around the hut. For so long they had existed in a male only world. In the two years since Aaron had been sentenced he'd been with men. Only men had been imprisoned on the hulk and the ship out here. Since then, the only woman he'd seen at a distance was Dan Wilkins', the old overseer's, wife. Having a constant feminine presence in their hut was strange and he found his mind constantly wandered to thoughts of them. It was unnerving.

Now that Lawrie was on the mend, however, thoughts returned to Jacob's new overseer, and when they could pay him a visit.

"I say we go tonight," said Paddy checking their supplies. "We're just about out of flour an' tea, an' there ain't much salt pork left."

"Aye we need ter get outta here," said Mick who had been getting a bit feverish being confined to the hut for the last week.

"Awright you'll git no argument from me," said Riley grinning at them. "We'll go after supper tonight."

"I wonder if he's fixed the lock on the door after you shot it off," said Aaron thoughtfully. "Twill make it easier to break in if he hasn't."

"Well even he has, we'll just shoot it off again," said Paddy laughing.

After supper, the four men armed themselves with muskets and pistols and set off for Jacob's farm. They left Lawrie at the hut in the care of Killara and Lowanna. They seemed to have learned a few English words and they had picked up a couple of their words as well. Although Aaron had to concede it was a lot easier to converse with them when Birrani was there.

They headed west from the hut along the wallaby track and crossed the river at Wallis Plains. They followed the river north skirting around McLeod's farmhouse. They expected him to be on alert and had no intention of having another shoot out if it could be avoided. They continued until they saw Jacob's overseer's house through the trees. Light was flickering in the window; someone was home.

They sheltered behind some nearby Lilly pilly bushes while they surveyed the scene. Aaron pressed his lips together as he watched the house and wondered how many were inside. Not knowing exactly what they might be facing always made him nervous.

"Do yer reckon he's alone?" asked Riley.

"Hard ter say," said Paddy scratching his head. "How about Aaron an' me go around ter the back door, an' yer an' Mick take the front."

Riley nodded. "Aye sounds good. Shoot off the lock an' we'll rush him."

"Awright. Come on," he said nudging Aaron.

They left the cover of the bushes and quietly crossed the yard and snuck down the side of the house. Aaron's heart was thumping loud in his ears, but he didn't think he could hear any voices coming from the house. That was a good sign. He was probably alone.

Paddy took his pistol from his belt as they approached the back door. He sucked in a deep breath and as soon as he let it out he fired his pistol. Aaron was pretty sure he'd hit the lock as it had made a metal pinging sound. He immediately shoved his shoulder into the door and it swung open and he and Paddy rushed into the house. No more than a second later he heard the lock on the front door shatter as well. By the time he righted himself enough to look around Paddy already had his pistol pointing at the head of a man who he presumed to be Richard Hines, the new overseer. Aaron hoped he didn't realise Paddy's pistol had already discharged and wasn't loaded.

Aaron quickly glanced around the room. There was no one else; it would appear that Hines was alone. Mick headed off into the bedroom to check for any other inhabitants but returned moments later shaking his head.

Richard gaped around at them. He was in his nightshirt, clearly about to retire for the evening, and Aaron smirked at the sight of him. He was a short sallow man with lank greasy black hair which was hanging limply. He had rather beady little eyes which were now darting from one to other as he nervously licked his lips.

"How dare ye!" he said at last with more bravado than he appeared.

Riley laughed. "Oh, we dare Dick. May I call yer Dick?"

"No, ye may not!"

Paddy chuckled. "I hope yer got some decent supplies, Dick," he said opening the larder and peering in. "Oh, good yer got tea an' flour." He took both as well as a cask of salt pork and a bag of peas.

"See if he's got any firearms," said Riley waving his pistol in Dick's face. "Sit down Dick."

He blustered but complied by sitting down in the nearest chair. Mick headed back into the bedroom to search for anything of value, while Riley kept a close eye on Dick. Aaron noticed a copy of the Australian newspaper on the table and reached for it. He scanned the front page for anything of interest, before folding it and shoving it in his pocket. A few minutes later Mick came back carrying a pair of pistols and a pocket watch.

"Well thank yer for bein' so obligin'," said Riley grinning at Dick. "Come on lads let's git outta here."

They loaded themselves up with supplies and Aaron swung open the front door and they stepped out into the cool night air. He paused to listen for anyone approaching before they set off for their hut. It had been a quick raid and Jacob's farm wasn't far from their hut, they'd be back there well before midnight.

~

Chapter Sixteen

Don McLeod's Homestead

Don McLeod was asleep with his wife Ann breathing softly by his side. It took a few minutes for him to realise that the loud banging wasn't in his dream, but that someone was thumping loudly on his front door. He awoke with a sudden fright and automatically leapt out of bed before his brain had even registered what he was doing.

"Shit," he exclaimed as he stubbed his toe on the nightstand.

The banging continued and was now accompanied by frantic yelling. "Mr McLeod!"

"I'm coming," he yelled back.

"What is it?" said Ann sitting up and peering around in the darkness.

"Go back to sleep," said Don throwing on his dressing gown. "Some idiot's banging on our door."

"Oh," she said ignoring his advice and climbing out of bed.

It was a dark night, but Don knew his house well enough. He grabbed his pistol from the dressing table before hurrying down the hall to the front door.

"Who is it? I warn you I'm armed."

"Tis me, Richard Hines, an' I'm not armed."

"Oh," replied Don unlocking the door and swinging it open. "What's the matter?"

"Tis the bushrangers," he said breathlessly as he just about fell into the house. "They bloody robbed me not fifteen minutes ago, I came as fast as I could." He was panting and gasping for air as he stepped over the threshold.

By this time Ann had arrived on the scene in her dressing gown, and she gaped open-mouthed at Richard. "Oh, Don you don't think they'll come here do you?" There was fear in her voice as she clutched her gown.

"Don't worry my dear, we'll catch them. Go back to bed."

"I can't possibly go back to bed!"

"Alright," said Don running his fingers through his hair. "Mr Hines, please wait here with my wife while I dress and we'll go in pursuit." He handed him his pistol. "Don't hesitate to shoot."

He raced back up the hall to the bedroom and quickly dressed. He returned not ten minutes later armed with a musket and pistol. He kissed Ann on the cheek. "Lock the door and don't let anyone in."

He could see the terror in her eyes as she breathed in heavily through her nose. "You can't leave me!"

"I must if we hope to bring an end to these outlaws," he said opening the door. "Come Mr Hines. I trust you know how to saddle a horse? I'll go fetch my overseer while you prepare our mounts. Come."

The two men hurried from the house, and Don was pleased when he heard the solid thump of his front door closing. He knew Ann was scared, but he could do nothing to ease her fears at the moment. Don showed Richard to the barn where the saddles and bridles were kept. Bales of hay muffled any sounds in the barn and all was quiet except for a startled neigh from the mare in the nearest stall.

"I'll be back to help you," he said over his shoulder as he left to fetch George McIntire.

The overseer's house was set back from the main house, away from the river. There was a dirt path which led to both the convict huts and the overseer's house from the rear garden. He rushed through the garden pausing to open the gate before continuing down the path. He stepped onto the narrow veranda of the overseer's house and hammered loudly on the door.

"George, it's me, Don," he called as he knocked.

His heartbeat had quickened and he could feel the thrum of adrenalin in his veins as he waited. He badly wanted to capture the outlaws and bring an end to their exploits. He knocked loudly on the door again and waited impatiently.

Finally, the door opened and a bleary-eyed George McIntire filled the doorway with his pistol pointed straight at Don's chest. He immediately dropped his arm when he realised who it was.

"Ah sorry," he mumbled.

"It's fine, not to worry," said Don brushing his apology aside. "Jacob's mob has just robbed Vic's new overseer and we need to go in pursuit. Quickly get dressed and meet us at the barn."

"Aye, sir."

Don turned on his heel and left. He was breathing heavily by the time he returned to help Richard who had one horse saddled, and another bridled. By the time George arrived they had three horses saddled and ready to go.

"We'll try and pick up the trail from Jacob's," said Don as he mounted his horse.

"I reckon they came this way," said Richard swinging up into the saddle. "South across the river."

"Really? We'll head for Wallis Plains then," said Don urging his horse into a trot.

The three men headed south from McLeod's farm following the river to the bridge. They were not likely to hear anything above the thud of hooves, and it was hard to see too far ahead. If they were going to have any luck finding them at all,

Don thought they'd just stumble across them. If they had no luck tonight, he'd enlist the assistance of Alexander Scott and mount a proper search party in the morning.

They reached the bridge across the Hunter River without seeing any sign of them. Don kicked his horse into a canter as they crossed the river and continued down the road. He was just wondering which way to go when he noticed a well-worn wallaby trail heading west. He brought his horse to a halt and waved to his companions.

"This looks like a likely trail," he said indicating the rough wallaby track which appeared to lead down to the Wallis Creek.

The other two nodded in agreement, and Don urged his mount forward and began to trot down the trail. His horse was sure footed and well used to the rough countryside, so he kicked it into a canter as they rushed headlong down the track. They followed it for a mile or so, and without finding any sign of the outlaw's Don came to a stop. He'd quickly come to the realisation that it was a useless waste of time trying to find them in the dark without trackers.

"I think we ought to call it a night," he said turning in his saddle to speak with George and Richard who had come to a halt behind him. "We're not going to find them in the dark."

"Aye we need trackers," said George nodding in agreement.

Richard reluctantly agreed and the three turned their horses for home.

~

Aaron let out the breath he'd been holding as the thud of horses hooves receded. He remained crouched down behind the large bottlebrush with Mick. Riley and Paddy were well out of sight hiding behind the bushes on the other side of the track. They hadn't had much time to find cover. No sooner had Aaron heard the sound of horses coming than they were upon them. They'd all dived under the bushes by the side of the track just in time. Aaron was thankful it was such a dark night or the outcome may have been quite different.

They waited crouched behind the bushes for several minutes until they were sure their pursuers were gone. At least Aaron presumed they were looking for them. Why else would several men on horseback be careening through the bush at this hour? Riley was the first one to emerge from the bushes.

"I think they're gone," he said looking up and down the track.

The rest of them came out of their hiding spots and joined him. Paddy was breathing heavily as he peered into the darkness.

"Shit that was close," he said shifting the bag of peas onto his shoulder. "That bloody Dick must've run fer help as soon as he could."

"Aye, we should've tied him up," put in Mick.

Riley nodded. "Too late now. Come on let's git outta here."

All was quiet and dark as they approached their hut. Clearly, the native women and Lawrie were already abed and they quietly crept inside. The fire had been dampened down but the coals were still glowing, and the whole hut smelled of camphor and turpentine.

Aaron was anxious to read the newspaper he'd taken from Hines, but it would have to wait until morning. He rolled himself up in his blanket and tried to go to sleep. He was tired, but his mind was wandering. He was surprised at how quickly he'd got used to raiding the settler's houses and robbing them. It seemed so long ago that he'd done his first burglary with James Barton back in Oxford.

He'd waited nervously while James disappeared through the gate and into Robinson's back garden. He pressed his back firmly against the stone wall so as to stay in the shadows. It was a moonless night though and he thought he'd be unnoticed even if somebody walked right passed him. He took in several deep breaths and shifted his weight to his other foot. He tightened his grip on the hessian sack he was carrying and felt for his knife which he'd jammed into his belt. Its worn handle felt solid and its presence reassured him.

James couldn't have been gone for more than five minutes, but time seemed to drag. He glanced up and down the street. All was quiet – there was no sign of anyone. He thought it must be getting onto 1 o'clock, and the night watchman would be doing his rounds in the next half hour or so. He took several deep breaths to calm his rising anxiety.

A minute later James' head popped out from behind the gate. "It's all clear. Come on," he whispered ducking back into the Robinson's garden.

Aaron took one last glance up and down the street before following him. It was even darker in the small garden, but he managed to make out James' dark shape ahead of him. They followed the stone path passed the wash house to the back of the house.

It was a two-story stone house and had several windows opening out onto the rear garden. All the downstairs windows were firmly secured with timber shutters. Aaron dropped the bag beside one of the windows close to the back door. He gestured to James that this looked like a suitable place to break in.

James nodded and immediately set to work with the brace and bit. It didn't take him long to bore several holes in the shutter. Aaron waited patiently, listening intently for any sound that someone was coming. He knew the Robinson's were not at home, but still, they needed to be quiet.

As soon as James had a hole large enough to fit his fingers through he gave the tools back to Aaron. He reached in, undid the bolt and the shutters sprang open. Aaron grinned at him and withdrew his knife. He carefully slid the blade in between the window sashes until he managed to push open the pivot catch. Jamming his knife back into his belt he wrenched open the window and climbed in. James was right behind him and he heard the soft thud of him dropping their bag on the floor. A few moments later the soft glow from a candle filled the kitchen.

Aaron had an odd feeling standing in someone else's kitchen uninvited. He looked about nervously. "Let's get what we can and get the hell out of here," he whispered to James.

"Aye."

He followed James and the small glow from the candle as they made their way through to the front of the house. A narrow stair ran up to the second floor and the bedrooms. At the top of the stair was a short hall which led to the master bedroom at the front of the house.

As he entered the room Aaron quickly looked about trying to see in the dim candlelight. There were several dark shapes and on the far wall Aaron could just make out a large wardrobe and he headed straight for it. He opened the doors and gestured James to bring the candle closer. The top shelf contained a number of hats which Aaron quickly removed and shoved into their bag. James was already opening the other wardrobe which likewise contained several fine hats.

Aaron pulled open several drawers and rummaged through the contents. He tossed most of this onto the floor as he hurriedly searched for anything of value.

"Come on," said James picking up their bag and heading for the door.

"Just a minute," said Aaron searching through one final drawer. He pulled out a fine-looking pocket watch and grinned at James. "We'll get a few pounds for this."

"Alright, but let's go."

They headed back down the narrow stairs and into the kitchen. James noticed a couple of leather aprons hanging on a hook. He grabbed them and tucked them into the bag before handing it to Aaron and climbing back out the window.

"Come on," said James waving his hands at Aaron to pass him the bag through the open window.

Aaron didn't need any further encouragement. He shoved the bag through the window to James and climbed out into the cold night air. He was so relieved to be out of the house. He gulped in several deep breaths before following James back down the path to the gate. They were just about at the gate when someone on the other side closed it. Aaron froze.

"What business do have there?" demanded a man's voice from the other side.

"What business do you have," replied James grabbing hold of the handle and giving the gate a wrench. It didn't budge.

"I know you've no business being in Mr Robinson's garden at this hour," came the voice. "Watchman! – Watchman!" he called down the street.

"Fuck!" exclaimed James handing Aaron their bag of goods as he tried once more to open the gate. It had obviously been secured from the other side and try as he might it remained firmly shut.

Aaron's heart was beating so hard in his ears that he couldn't think straight. He glanced around the dark garden. He couldn't see a damn thing. The garden wall was at least eight feet high all the way around. They wouldn't be able to scale that. They were trapped like a pair of rats.

"Come on. There must be a way we can climb this wall," said James heading down among the shrubbery. "We need to get out of here afore he gets back with the watch."

Aaron followed him. There were no grab holds on the stone wall, and they searched for a tree or shrub close to it that they could climb. Panic gripped Aaron as they searched the garden for a way out. The minutes flew by as they desperately searched for an escape route. James tried to scale the wall with his bare hands, but he had to give up. There was no way out.

"When they come through that gate be ready to jump 'em," said James as they made their way back up the garden to the gate. "We can give 'em the slip."

"Aye," replied Aaron. He was surprised at how calm his voice sounded; he sure as hell didn't feel calm. He dropped the bag and shoved it under a nearby bush. He didn't want to be encumbered with that when the time came.

As they waited the darkness seemed to envelope Aaron. Every breath was loud in his ears as he strained to hear what was happening on the other side of the fence. It wasn't long before he heard footsteps hurrying towards them. It sounded like several people were coming. Every muscle tensed as he prepared to rush at whoever opened the damn gate.

"In here - in here. I've got 'em locked in the garden."

Scuffling noises were coming from the other side of the gate like rope was being untied and pulled through a metal bolt. A moment later the gate was pushed forcefully open and two men rushed into the garden. Aaron immediately sprang to his feet and rushed forward with James pushing him from behind.

He felt rough hands grab him around the waist and a shoulder was shoved into his belly. He instinctively grabbed the man around the shoulders as they were both propelled backwards into the garden. He lost his footing and fell hard with the man landing on top of him. He could feel his hot breath panting in his ear as he gasped for air.

"I've got one of 'em buggers," he yelled pushing hard down on Aaron's shoulders, pinning him to the ground.

Aaron struggled and kicked as he tried to push him off. He heard James give a loud grunt as though he'd been badly winded and he wrestled harder with his assailant to escape his grasp. He dug his fingers hard into the man's ribs until he released him with a yelp. He quickly rolled to one side and scrambled to his feet. The air had been pushed from his lungs when the man had landed on top of him and he gasped as he gulped in several large breaths.

He paused for no more than a second before he started running for the open gate. He was almost there when two large arms wrapped around his knees. He sprawled face-first onto the street, and this time the wind was completely knocked out of him. He wheezed as he tried to suck in a lungful of air, but it was too late. The man grabbed his arms wrenching them behind his back; at the same time, he pressed his knee hard into his back with all his weight.

"I got 'im this time," he called breathless to his companion.

"Good," came the reply. "Hang onto him this time."

Aaron lay there gasping for air while the man trussed him up like a turkey. Adrenalin was still pumping through his veins but fear gripped him. It was like a living thing that snaked around his intestines and made his insides squirm. They would hang for sure.

~

Chapter Seventeen

The Hut, Spark's Farm

The following morning Lawrie was much improved and even joined in on the conversation about their close shave the previous night. Killara was about to apply a fresh poultice of leaves and bark to Lawrie's shoulder when Aaron went over to take a closer look. Around the wound was still a bit red and swollen, but there was no sign of blood or pus. There was new pink skin around the outer edge and the sickly sweet odour had all but gone.

"It looks good," he said smiling at Lawrie.

"Aye, Killara has saved me life without a doubt," replied Lawrie. "I reckon I'll be well enough ter join yer on yer next raid."

"Hmm maybe," said Riley looking at him. "Perhaps yer can go an' scout for a likely target. Yer don't want ter over do it."

Lawrie nodded and smiled at Killara as she applied the concoction to his wound. "Thank yer."

She smiled at him in return and got to her feet. She said something to Lowanna in her own language. She nodded and opened the door and waited for Killara to exit. They both left, closing the door behind them. No one paid them any attention. The women were free to come and go as they pleased, which they often did. They would return later in the day with fresh leaves and bark. Birrani might even join them and bring yams and other edible plants.

Paddy filled the now empty billy with water. He smelled it as he put the lid on and screwed up his nose. "The tea is gonna taste like camphor," he said as he hung it on the hook over the fire.

"Sorry about that," said Lawrie shrugging.

Aaron turned his attention to the newspaper he'd taken last night. He unfolded it and scanned the front page. There wasn't much of interest so he turned the page; looking for any mention of them or other newsworthy items. It took him a minute to realise that the others were staring at him.

"What?" he said raising a dark brow as he looked at them.

"Can yer read?" said Paddy peering at the newspaper.

Aaron eyed them warily. "Aye. Can't you?"

"Good God no. I ain't never had any schoolin'."

"Me either," said Lawrie. "My Da always said it twas a waste of time."

Riley and Mick nodded in agreement with Paddy. Apparently, none of them could read or write. Aaron realised that he should have known. They were farmers for the most part and would not need to know their letters.

"What does it say?" asked Riley clearly curious.

"Well not much," said Aaron turning the page again. "I thought there might be something in here about us." He continued to scan the page. He'd half expected them to be mentioned. They'd be listed as absconded convicts if nothing else, but so far there had been no mention. He turned the page again and that's when he noticed the small advertisement.

"Oh here we go," he said grinning at them. "Spark is offering a sixty dollar reward for your apprehension. Twenty dollars each for Riley, Lawrie and Paddy. Apparently, we aren't worth anything Mick."

"What! Nothing for us at all?"

"No, I'm afraid not."

"And here we are right under his very nose. We're on his land," said Riley laughing.

"Aye," said Paddy chuckling. "Twenty dollars for me though, that's a good sum."

"Well I'm glad you're happy about it," said Aaron as he continued to look for any other items of interest. He turned the page. "Oh, here's a whole piece about us."

"What does it say?" said Lawrie eager for more.

"Well for one thing they think we're hiding at Narrow Gut. It mentions you, Lawrie," he said looking up at him. "It says how Dr Radford wounded one of us and they found your bloodied waistcoat. They think they'll have us captured any day now," he said grinning at them. "They've got no idea where we are."

They all laughed at that news.

"It also says here that the natives are refusing to track for them," he said. "Of course we knew that, but it's good to know."

"Aye," said Riley. "An' ter think Paddy was worried they'd tell them where we were."

"Well that was when we first met them," said Paddy defensively. "I trust them now."

"Well I reckon we need ter gather some information," said Riley brushing aside talk of the natives. "I'd like ter pay back any of them buggers who've been helpin' Scott an' McLeod. We also need some good items for trade an' such. Any ideas?"

"Well I want ter be in on it, an' if yer will not let me come with yer, at least let me, scout," said Lawrie getting to his feet to demonstrate how well he was. He swayed slightly and leaned against the wall to steady himself. "I'm awright."

"Oh aye sure yer are," scoffed Paddy.

"I need ter do something," insisted Lawrie.

"Let him come with us," put in Mick looking Lawrie up and down. "Twill help him get his strength back."

"I'll go as well," said Aaron folding up the newspaper. "Mick and I'll take care of him."

"Awright," said Paddy begrudgingly. He took the billy from the fire and poured in some tea leaves and left it to brew. "Anyone for tea? It'll taste like camphor mind."

They all nodded. Aaron didn't care about the tea tasting funny. He was excited to be going out scouting and collecting information. He agreed with Riley. They needed to do something big again like when they burnt Reid's house down. But they needed help. Most of the convicts were happy to aid them and give information, as long as their master's were being harassed and attacked. Aaron didn't think that had been going so well of late, and they really needed a good raid to put the fear back into the settlers. He was excited at the prospect.

~

It was late morning when Mick, Aaron and Lawrie left the hut. They were dressed in regular clothes so as to appear like free men. They were armed with muskets and pistols and Paddy had given them a couple of Johnny cakes each for their midday meal. It was early spring, and pale sunshine was peeking out from between the light fluffy clouds. Aaron took in a deep breath and sighed.

The three men headed east from their hut along the wallaby trail. They hoped to run into some croppies and gather what information they could. The township of Wallis Plains was situated near the bridge, and they skirted around it and continued heading eastward. They passed through William Harper's property, but there were no sign of any work gangs.

The next farm along belonged to Lesley Duguid. The main road cut through the middle of it and they kept to the north by the river. Aaron came to a halt by a stand of cedar trees and listened.

"Do you hear that? Sounds like someone sawing nearby."

"Aye I hear it," said Lawrie peering through the trees.

They went on a little further; all the while keeping an eye out for whoever was doing the sawing. Aaron knew it would be croppies. The question was, were they alone or not. They followed the sound until finally, Aaron spotted two croppies, one on each end of a cross-cut saw. They were cutting down a large acacia tree. He didn't think they'd spotted them.

He looked through the trees to see if there was anyone else around. They waited, hidden behind a large bottlebrush to see if anyone else would appear.

"I reckon they're alone," whispered Mick.

"Aye," said Lawrie peering through the shrubs.

Aaron sucked in a deep breath and waited; watching for another minute or so before he was convinced their overseer wasn't nearby. "Alright."

The three of them stepped out from behind the bushes and approached the two men. They stopped work and glanced quickly at one another before turning their attention to the three interlopers. They eyed them warily.

"What do ye want?" said one of them. He was young with a mop of ginger hair which was sticking out from under his cap. The other one stared at them with intense blue eyes.

"You might have heard of us," said Aaron smiling. His smile belied the nervous flutter in his belly, and he hoped the men wouldn't notice his bravado. "We're members of the Jacob's mob, and we're after some information about your master."

"We don't want any trouble," said the blue-eyed one.

"We ain't gonna give yer any trouble," said Lawrie. "I'm Lawrie, this is Aaron an' Mick."

"I'm Ed, an' that's Joe," said the ginger-haired one.

"Nice to meet you," said Aaron. Again he smiled at them in the hope that would lessen their concerns. "So, you're assigned to Duguid are you?"

"Aye," said Joe still eyeing them warily.

"We're thinkin' of robbin' him," said Mick. "Who's your overseer?"

"John Roberts. He's away, an' Martin Dealy's taken over," said Joe. "Dealy's alright."

He seemed to relax slightly but Aaron noticed he licked his lips, which he read as apprehension.

"You can trust us," he said in an effort to reassure them. "How does this John Robert's treat you?"

A look of caution passed between them. Aaron sighed. He didn't seem to be getting anywhere.

"I promise yer he won't find out," said Lawrie. "An' if he does it'll be ter late." He laughed.

"We're gonna rob him even if yer don't tell us anythin'," said Mick shrugging.

The two men looked at one another and Aaron let out his breath. He thought that was a look that meant they would trust them.

"Aye Dealy's not the problem," said Ed. "It's Robert's that's put us on short rations an' such. But he ain't here."

"Well we'll take care of him when he gets back," said Lawrie. "What about Duguid? Has he got anythin' worth stealin' do yer know?"

Joe glanced at Ed and then gave a slight nod.

"What's in it for us?" said Ed looking interested.

Lawrie smiled. "What do yer want? Extra food rations, blankets or maybe a firearm. Yer tell us an' we'll see what we can do."

"What do ye reckon?" said Ed looking at Joe.

"I reckon some provisions an' extra blankets would be worth it."

"It's a deal," said Aaron. "So tell us what do you know."

Joe nodded. "Duguid's in Sydney an' won't be back for another week or more. He's just had a fresh load of provisions delivered."

"Really," said Lawrie nodding. "Sounds like there'll be a lot of food ter take. We might need help ter carry it away."

"Aye," put in Mick. "What about valuables? Any idea what he's got?"

"Aye," said Ed. "I've seen him with a pair of pocket pistols. An' him bein' a surveyor an' all, he's got a compass. He keeps it in a small wooden box."

"He's got a nice silver pocket watch as well," said Joe. "I don't think he was wearin' it when he left."

"Thank yer gentlemen, you've been very helpful," said Lawrie grinning. "Sounds like twill be a good haul."

"When are ye goin' to do it?" asked Ed.

"Probably in a night or two. I'm sure you'll hear all about it," said Aaron smiling. "And don't worry, we'll find you and give you your share."

"Come on lads, we'll need ter take a look at the house an' see how the land lies," said Lawrie.

"It's just north of here, down near the river. Ye cannot miss it," said Joe.

The three of them headed off in the direction that Joe had indicated. The house was only a few hundred yards further on, set back from the river bank. It was a large homestead with a wide veranda along the front which had a vine climbing over part of it. A large barn was situated to one side of the front yard which had a small paddock beside it.

Aaron, Mick and Lawrie concealed themselves behind a large grevillea and surveyed the scene. It was quiet, and Aaron didn't think anyone was around. Still, they didn't want Dealy alerted to their intentions.

"We should be able ter creep up ter the front door without being seen," said Lawrie. "We can use the cover of the barn."

Aaron agreed. "Alright, let's head back and tell Paddy and Riley," he said. "You can bet Riley will want to come back tonight."

"Aye particularly when 'e 'ears about the pistols," said Lawrie chuckling. His breath caught, and he coughed several times before he managed to catch his breath again.

"Are you alright," asked Aaron concern creasing his brow.

He exchanged a worried look with Mick. Lawrie wasn't anywhere near back to full strength, and Aaron thought today had probably been too much for him.

"I'm fine," said Lawrie gasping.

He didn't seem to be alright. He'd gone red in the face and he was trembling. Aaron handed him a canteen of water.

"Drink."

He took a large draft of water and then handed the canteen back to Aaron.

"Thank yer. I'm alright."

"We best head back," said Mick casting a worried look at Lawrie.

~

Chapter Eighteen

Duguid's Homestead

It was the following afternoon before the men armed themselves ready to raid Duguid's farm. They'd spent the previous evening coming up with a plan to surprise Martin Dealy, the acting overseer.

"I'll be fine, I wanna come," said Lawrie visibly frustrated.

"Yesterday took a lot ert of yer. We can't be worrying about yer," said Riley shoving a pistol in his belt. "Stay here Lawrie, for yer own sake as well as ours."

He was being stubborn. Aaron suspected he bloody well knew it would be too much for him. After their scouting mission yesterday he'd been exhausted. He'd retired early and had only roused himself when Killara and Lowanna had returned. He'd been arguing with Riley all day, and Aaron was sick of hearing it.

"I'll meet you outside," he finally said to Riley. He stepped out into the mid-afternoon sun and took in a deep breath. He was equally nervous and excited about tonight's raid. Things had gone so badly at Radford's, and even though they'd successfully raided Jacob's new overseer, they'd had a close call with whoever had pursued them. He hoped tonight would go without a hitch.

A few minutes later Paddy and Mick joined him. "They're still arguing," said Paddy groaning. "He's just being bloody stubborn."

"Well if Riley doesn't hurry up, we'll go without him as well," said Mick. "I just wanna get on with it."

Paddy and Aaron nodded. They agreed with Mick's assessment.

It was another five minutes before the door to the hut opened and Riley came out. "That's the end of it, Lawrie," he said over his shoulder. "I'll bloody shoot yer meself if yer don't quit." He sighed. "Come on let's go."

The four men set off heading east towards Wallis Plains. A cool breeze was blowing but Aaron thought it would be a dry evening. The sky was overcast with patches of blue and every now and then the sun shone between the clouds. It was only a couple of miles to Duguid's homestead and he expected they'd get there on dusk. A mob of wallabies bounded out of the bush ahead of them and startled him. He had his pistol halfway out of his belt before he realised they were just wallabies. He grinned at Mick who had stopped just ahead of him, clearly surprised by the animals.

The sun was low in the sky as they approached Duguid's homestead. The yard looked deserted and Aaron suspected no one was home. Well, Dealy would get a surprise when he arrived and they were waiting for him. They were halfway across the yard heading for the shelter of the barn when they noticed two men. The men had been out of sight as they approached and Aaron hadn't noticed anyone until they were almost upon them. They were stacking timber by the side of the barn and looked up at the same time.

Aaron froze and glanced at Riley. He kept on walking as though nothing was out of the ordinary. Aaron knew this wasn't the plan, but he quickly regained his composure and went along with Riley's charade.

"Good evenin'," said Riley. "Have yer heard anythin' of the bushrangers?"

A tall lanky looking man put the log he was holding on the pile before turning to face Riley. "No."

There was no alarm on the man's thin face. He obviously thought they were searching for the bushrangers. Perhaps he thought they were after the reward money that Sharp was offering. Whatever was going through the man's mind, it clearly hadn't occurred to him that they were the bushrangers. The other man paid them no attention at all. He went on stacking the wood. Aaron smiled inwardly. What idiots.

"Thank yer," replied Riley. He very casually turned and took a couple of steps away from the men. His grey eyes were steely as he looked from Mick, Paddy and Aaron to the house and back again. He made the slightest nod of his head and repeated the movement with his eyes.

It dawned on Aaron at the same time that the others realised what he wanted them to do. The four of them headed for the veranda and rushed into the house. The front door opened into the parlour which was small and overstuffed with furniture. A large sideboard took up one whole wall. Two rooms went off from here; one to the left and one to the right. A short hall, which presumably led to the kitchen out back, was the only other exit.

"Grab all the firearms," said Riley over his shoulder as he hurried into the room on the right.

Aaron could hear yells of surprise coming from the men outside and knew they'd be upon them within seconds. Mick had already headed off down the hall, and Paddy was searching the parlour. Aaron hurried into the other room to search for any weapons. It looked like a guest room with a large bed taking up most of the available space and an armoire squeezed up against one wall. He quickly scanned the room for weapons. It didn't look like there were any so he rushed back out into the parlour just as the two men came through the front door.

"What the hell?" said the tall lanky one, astonishment written all over his face.

Aaron whipped his pistol from his belt and pointed it directly at the man's chest. Paddy was right beside him with his musket at his shoulder pointing at the other man.

"Where's the pocket pistols?" asked Aaron brandishing his weapon at them.

"What?"

"Come now, yer know what we're talking about," said Paddy.

Riley came back into the parlour carrying a blunderbuss and a musket. "Is this all the firearms?"

The two men quickly recovered from their surprise. The one who Aaron thought must be Dealy – he was doing all the talking, had recovered his senses. He stared at them as he appeared to be assessing the situation; weighing up the odds perhaps. Aaron relaxed his grip on the pistol slightly when the man's shoulders slumped.

"In the chest in there," he said pointing to the room Riley had just vacated. "Hidden under the clothes."

Riley dropped the blunderbuss and musket by the front door and headed back into the room with Paddy at his side.

"Move down the hall to the kitchen," said Aaron flicking the pistol left and right. "I reckon you can cook us supper. Move."

They walked cautiously ahead of Aaron down the short hall. Mick was ransacking the larder and already had sacks of flour, sugar and tea which he'd piled near the door ready for them to take. He looked up and grinned as the two men entered with Aaron.

"These two are going to cook us supper," said Aaron keeping his pistol aimed at them.

"Oh good, I'm starvin'," said Mick. "Where's Riley an' Paddy?"

"They're searching for the pistols."

"What about the compass?"

"I'd forgotten about that. Where is it?" said Aaron.

"In the parlour," said Dealy dumping a sack of turnips on the table. "In the sideboard. It's in a small box in the bottom drawer."

"I'll go get it," said Mick and he disappeared down the hall.

Dealy and his offsider set about preparing supper without complaint. The kitchen was quite large with a table in the middle and a dresser against one wall. The well stocked larder was actually a small room off the kitchen. Along one wall was a trough and bench which had a keg of water sitting on it. The hearth and wood stove took up the opposite side of the kitchen.

Riley, Paddy and Mick returned about twenty minutes later, with the pistols and compass. They dumped them on the floor beside the sacks along with a silver thimble and a fancy pocket watch. The smell of pork stew was already permeating the kitchen, and Riley tilted his nose in the air and breathed in.

"How long will supper be? I'm starvin'."

"Not long," said Dealy looking sourly at Riley. "Ye really fooled me ye did."

"Aye. I can't believe yer fell for it," he said grinning. "Have yer found any wine or spirits?"

"No," replied Mick sitting down at the table.

"Ye know they wants to hang ye don't ye?" said Dealy getting bowls out of the dresser and placing them on the table. "They'll have the soldiers out after ye for sure."

Aaron glanced at Riley. His steely grey eyes had narrowed and he was eyeing Dealy like he'd like to hit him. He didn't have to. Paddy swung around and slammed his fist into the side of Dealy's head. Dealy grunted in surprise and stumbled. He grabbed the side of his face and took a couple of steps before he righted himself.

"Shut up," growled Paddy.

The other man was about to ladle the stew into the bowls. He froze and stared at them.

"Aye," said Riley glaring at Dealy. "'Tis best yer don't comment on such things."

Dealy sucked in a deep breath and glared at Paddy, but said nothing else. He nodded to the other man and he proceeded to spoon the stew into the bowls. Aaron took his bowl of stew and began eating. It wasn't bad, but Paddy was a better cook than these two. He unobtrusively peered at Paddy. He was eating his supper, and looking like nothing had happened. Riley was still eyeing the two men warily. For the first time, Aaron wondered if he could trust his companions.

They finished their supper in relative quiet.

"See if yer can find some rope," said Riley rising to his feet. "We'll need ter tie this pair up afore we leave. We don't want ter find ourselves bein' chased again."

Dealy showed no emotion at these words.

Paddy set off to the barn to find some rope. In the meantime, Riley went to fetch the two guns while Aaron kept an eye on their prisoners. Paddy returned a few minutes later with two lengths of coarse rope. He handed one to Mick and they tied up the two men and secured them each to a chair.

They each grabbed a sack of supplies and the valuables before heading off back to their hut. It wasn't late. Aaron thought it was probably only around eight o'clock as they began to make their way back. He sighed. At least they wouldn't be pursued tonight. It would take a while before the two men freed themselves and raised the alarm.

~

Alexander Scott wasn't a tolerant man, and his patience had most definitely come to an end. Ten days ago he'd sent a request to Newcastle for fresh troops to hunt down the increasingly bold bushrangers. He was still waiting and growing more annoyed by the day. In the meantime the outlaws had robbed Lesley Duguid of a vast amount of supplies; enough to last them several weeks.

He'd just sat down to his midday meal when there was a knock at the door. Mary looked at him and was about to rise when he stopped her.

"No, no. Stay there I'll see who it is."

He stepped into the hall, and went to the front door and opened it.

"Corporal Higgins," he said scowling at him. "I hope you've got some bloody good news."

"Aye, sir. Captain Allman's arrived from Newcastle. He's brought a Sergeant Wilcox and four Privates with him. Should I send him around to see ye?"

They'd arrived at last - about bloody time. "No Corporal. I'll come down to the barracks," he said the crease in his brow easing. "Tell the Captain I'll be there directly."

"Aye, sir."

Alexander closed the door behind the Corporal and went back to finish his dinner.

"I take it that was Corporal Higgins?" said Mary when he returned.

"Aye. Captain Allman's arrived at last with fresh troops. Now we'll be able to get after those damn outlaws," said Alexander sitting back down at the table. "I do beg your pardon, Mary."

"Not at all," she said smiling at him. "I take it you'll be going with them then?"

"Aye." He wasn't particularly looking forward to being in the saddle for the next few weeks, but he wanted them buggers caught. With luck, it wouldn't take that long to find them. Although without native trackers they would have to rely on luck.

He finished his midday meal and kissed Mary goodbye. He packed extra clothes and provisions in his saddlebags; saddled his horse and set off down the road towards the barracks. It was less than half a mile to the barracks but he urged his mount into a canter. He couldn't wait to get there and organise the search.

He came to a halt outside the barracks and secured his horse to the hitching post. He could hear the sounds of men's voices coming from inside the barracks. He smiled to himself. The soldiers sounded as anxious to be out after the bushrangers as he was. He found Captain Allman and the fresh troops from Newcastle in the guard room.

"Captain Allman, I'm grateful that you've come," he said as he entered the room and spied the Captain. There were several other soldiers who he hadn't met before. He acknowledged them with a nod. "I'm afraid we don't have any trackers to assist us. The local natives are refusing to help in any way."

Captain Allman's brow creased into a frown. "Do ye have any idea where the bushrangers are hiding out then?"

"Some intelligence suggests they may be camped near Narrow Gut. To be honest with you Captain, we haven't had sight of them for weeks."

"We'll split into two search parties then," said Captain Allman. "Sergeant Wilcox, you take Privates Wilson and Smith with you. We'll take Privates Coffee and Wright with us."

Alexander considered this idea for a moment. He supposed that two smaller search parties would cover twice as much ground. He nodded. "Aye, that's a good idea Captain."

"Which way do ye want us to go?" asked Sergeant Wilcox.

Alexander was surprised by his deep gravelly voice. He wasn't a big man and his voice didn't really match him. He was a short reedy sort of man, and thin almost to the point of being gaunt.

"Ye take the north side of the river. Head northwest from the bridge. You'll have more luck if ye keep to the higher ground."

"Aye sir," replied Sergeant Wilcox before turning to Privates Wilson and Smith. "Ye heard the Captain, let's go." Sergeant Wilcox and the two Privates headed out of the barracks.

"Well if you're ready Captain," said Alexander, and not waiting for a response marched from the barracks. He could hear the Captain and Privates Coffee and Wright scrambling to catch up with him. He grimaced. He'd been out in pursuit with Allman before. He was no tracker, and he hoped to God either Coffee or Wright had some idea of how to read for signs. It was going to be a fruitless exercise otherwise.

He mounted his horse and waited for the rest of the party. It was already mid-afternoon, but he hoped they'd cover a few miles before they had to camp for the night. He sighed as he waited for them. The only positive he could see in all of this was the weather. They had clear skies and warm spring sunshine. Things could be worse.

~

Chapter Nineteen

Wallis Plains

Scott and his party had been scouring the bush for three days, and all they'd managed to do was scare a few wallabies. Alexander breathed in the cool morning air as he squatted by the smoky fire; a mug of tea clasped in his hands. He was frustrated at their lack of progress. He sighed as he tossed the last of his tea out and got to his feet. He stretched.

"I'll take ye cup sir," said Private Wright stretching his hand out towards him.

Alexander handed it over without looking at him. He was distracted with thoughts of which way they should go today. They'd searched east of Wallis Plains for the last three days without finding any trace of the bushrangers. Of course, he knew the majority of the croppies wouldn't tell them if they'd seen them, but he was convinced that most had told the truth. Yesterday they'd come across a small band of natives, but they'd been tight-lipped and noncommittal. He wondered why the natives had sided with the bushrangers.

"Are ye ready to go sir?" asked Private Wright as he stamped out the small fire. "Captain Allman's anxious to be under way."

Alexander glanced at the young freckle-faced Private. "Aye. Have you saddled my horse?"

"Aye, sir."

He turned to look. Sure enough, his horse was saddled and his bags were slung across her hindquarters. He walked over to his horse and checked the girth strap. Miranda was a sturdy young mare, but she had a tendency to blow her stomach out when she felt the girth strap being tightened. He unbuckled the strap and tightened it up one notch before swinging up into the saddle.

Captain Allman mounted his horse and sucked in a deep breath. He was a man of few words, and he gazed at Alexander, obviously waiting for him to give instructions. Alexander settled into the saddle and sighed.

"I think we ought to head west," he said at last. "We've had no luck this side of Wallis Plains."

"Aye," nodded Captain Allman. He clicked his tongue and urged his horse on.

Alexander and the two Privates fell into single file behind the Captain. They followed the creek westwards towards Wallis Plains, all the while alert for any sign of the outlaws. There wasn't a track along the creek as such, but the bare compacted earth gave the impression of a trail possibly used by the natives or the wildlife. Captain Allman kept to it until it petered out completely. He then turned north towards the river where the trees and shrubbery grew more sparse.

They continued through the sparsely vegetated edge of the river for most of the day. Apart from a few wallabies and birds, they saw no sign of the outlaws. Alexander was sure they'd be signs of where they'd camped if they'd been in the area, but there was no trace. He hoped Sergeant Wilcox was having more success.

It was late in the day when they stopped and made camp by the river under a wide shady gum tree. The weather was mild and fine, and there was plenty of dry timber around which Private Coffee collected for a fire. In no time at all the two young Privates had a stew of turnips and salt pork bubbling away over the fire.

Alexander rolled out his swag a short distance from the fire and after tending to his horse settled down on a fallen log. Captain Allman came and sat down on the end of the log with him.

"Tomorrow we should investigate Wallis Creek," he said pressing his lips together. "Ain't no sign they've been near the river." He shook his head to shoo away the flies that had landed on his face.

Alexander nodded and breathed out. "Aye, you might be right. I have to agree there's no sign they've been anywhere around these parts."

"Ye supper," said Private Wright handing each of them a bowl of stew with a chunk of dry bread.

Alexander and the Captain ate in silence. A slight breeze was blowing and bringing it with it the sound of screeching cockatoos as they settled on their roosts for the night. Alexander took another mouthful of stew and chewed slowly. Maybe tomorrow they'd have more luck in finding the outlaws. He bloody hoped so. He hated being out in the bush. Days in the saddle and uncomfortable nights sleeping on the hard ground always left him with cramped muscles and sore bones.

The following morning they set off early heading south away from the river. Captain Allman thought they'd pick up the Wallis Creek on the western side of Wallis Plains. It took them all morning wandering through the bush to find the creek. Alexander was annoyed with their progress; he was bloody sure they'd been going around in circles for hours, but the Captain wouldn't hear it. He came to a halt on the shallow creek bank and let Miranda drink her fill. It was quiet, with only the sound of a few birds and the gurgling of water in the creek.

"I suggest we follow the creek," said Alexander breathing heavily.

"Aye," replied Captain Allman pulling on the reins and coaxing his horse into a walk.

Alexander didn't know this part of the country, and he wasn't sure which side of Wallis Plains they were on. For the moment, he was content to follow the Captain. At least they were heading west and covering ground they hadn't searched before. They followed the creek for several miles without sighting anything of significance. It was when they stopped for their midday meal - which consisted of some cold stew from last night with a hard biscuit - that Alexander noticed a well-worn trail heading west along the creek.

"That looks like a likely track," he said pointing with his biscuit. "We should follow that after dinner."

Captain Allman gazed in the direction that he'd pointed and shrugged. "Looks like a wallaby trail tis all," he said unimpressed.

Alexander suppressed a grunt of frustration and bit into the piece of hard biscuit. The man was an idiot! He breathed in heavily through his nose as he attempted to squash his rising ire. It would do no good to start arguing amongst themselves. He finished his dinner in silence. He was seething by the time he remounted his horse and they set off. Alexander kicked Miranda into a trot and headed her down the wallaby trail. They'd only been following it for a couple of miles when he noticed a wisp of smoke rising through the cedar trees ahead. He came to a stop.

"That looks like smoke," he said twisting in his saddle so that he could speak with Captain Allman. "What do you think?"

"Aye. Probably natives," he said squinting to look through the trees.

It probably was natives, but he still thought it worth investigating. "We should take a closer look."

"Alright," said Captain Allman clicking his tongue to coax his mount on.

~

Aaron sighed and breathed in the aroma of roasting wallaby. Mick had shot it early this morning and Paddy had the hind on roasting for supper. He was also pleased that since their last raid the conversation about going to America had gained some ground.

"I reckon Aaron's right, we need ter get outta here," said Lawrie. "We ought ter head for the coast."

"I don't fancy stowin' away in the bilge of some ship," said Riley screwing up his face."How do yer expect us ter git on board?"

"Well, we could pay our fares," put in Mick. "We've got a few valuables we could sell or trade."

"And who would sell us passage? The bloody Governor has the harbour well under his control," said Riley shaking his head.

"Maybe a passin' whaler," said Paddy. "Let's just get ter the coast an' then we can work it ert."

"We should ask Birrani if he'll be our guide. Show us the way," said Aaron excitement clear in his hazel eyes.

"Awright," said Riley and he heaved a sigh of resignation. "Count me in. But I still say it's a damned risky idea."

They were so engrossed in their conversation that the sound of gunfire took them by complete surprise. A musket ball slammed into the side of the hut quickly followed by another.

"Holy shit!" exclaimed Paddy jumping to his feet.

Riley pulled his pistol from his belt as he opened the door and raced outside. Aaron was right behind him, but he stopped in the doorway as another musket ball slammed into the hut causing splinters of wood to fly off in all directions. Riley fired at two soldiers who'd just emerged from behind a cedar tree before running from the hut and sheltering behind an old stump.

Mick and Paddy squeezed out of the hut in between Aaron and the door frame. Riley stood up to fire another round but one of the soldiers fired first. The ball hit Riley in the eye.

"Aargh," he screamed dropping his pistol. He put his hand to his face and looked towards the hut where the others were watching; horrified. He dropped to the ground dead.

Mick and Paddy took off running for the cover of the cedar trees. Several shots were fired in their direction but they missed their mark. Lawrie raced out of the hut and paused to fire at the soldiers. His pistol burst in his hand, peeling back the barrel and leaving him with bits of the firearm embedded in his hand. He yelped, dropped the weapon and ran for cover.

Aaron's heart was thumping madly. Bloody hell! Riley was dead. He couldn't believe what he was seeing. One of the soldiers pointed his musket directly at his chest. He looked around wildly for the others, but they were gone. He dropped his pistol and raised his hands above his head in surrender. He gulped in several large lungfuls of air as he stared wide-eyed at Riley sprawled face-first in the dirt.

Two of the soldiers took off running after Mick, Paddy and Lawrie. The other grabbed Aaron roughly and put a pair of manacles on him before dragging him over to a nearby tree, which he tied him to with a length of rope. It all happened so fast it was a bit of a blur.

An older man emerged from the trees. Aaron presumed it was Alexander Scott. He was in civilian clothes and he walked over to where Riley was lying dead. He put his boot under Riley's body and turned him over onto his back. Where his eye had once been was now a bloody cavern with shards of bone showing where part of his face had been blown away. Aaron's stomach heaved and he swallowed the bile that soured the back of his throat. He turned away from the grisly sight.

"Where's Wright and Coffee?" asked the older man.

"They've gone after the three that got away," replied the soldier.

"Good," he said glancing at Aaron momentarily. "Keep an eye on him." He walked the few steps to the hut and went inside.

Aaron took in a deep breath and slowly let it out. He knew they'd be no escape this time, but he felt calm. He knew they'd hang him, but even that thought didn't send tremors of fear through him. He felt oddly resigned to his fate and almost welcomed it. In his heart, he'd always known their escapades would end badly. The likelihood of getting away to America had been nothing more than a dream, and now it was over.

About ten minutes later Scott came back out of the hut carrying the items they'd recently stolen from Duguid's. He had the compass and the case the pocket pistols were in. Aaron assumed he'd also found the silver pocket watch and other sundry items. It made no difference now.

He looked up as he heard men approaching. It was the two younger soldiers and they had Mick in their grasp. There was no sign of Paddy or Lawrie. He presumed they'd gotten away, although with Lawrie's shoulder and now his wounded hand he didn't think they'd get far.

"We got this one, but the other two got away," said the young freckle-faced soldier.

"Bring him over here," said the older soldier indicating to where Aaron was tied to the tree. He headed for the trees and came back moments later with a pair of manacles which he put on Mick. He then untied Aaron from the tree and tied him to Mick.

Mick locked eyes with Aaron but said nothing. Aaron couldn't read his face but thought he was trying to say the others hadn't gone far. He wondered if Paddy had been wounded as well.

"If you can take these two back to Wallis Plains, we'll search for the others," said the soldier to Scott.

"Aye, I can do that. Fetch my horse," he said turning to the young freckle-faced Private.

He immediately rushed off through the trees to fetch his horse and returned a few minutes later leading a chestnut mare. The older soldier grabbed the rope that Aaron and Mick were tied together with and gave it a tug.

"Get up."

They got their feet and he hauled them over to the horse and tied the rope to the pommel. They would have to walk or be dragged behind the animal. Aaron breathed in heavily through his nose as he tried to remain calm. It was bad enough being on a horse, but having to keep up with one as they traversed the bush while tied to Mick was going to take all his resolve.

"Tell Corporal Higgins not to remove the manacles from these two," said the soldier.

"Aye," said Scott as he swung up into the saddle. "I'll see him hung if he lets these two escape. Report back to me once you've got the other two in custody Captain."

"Aye."

He gave the horse a slight kick with his heels and it started walking, and Aaron and Mick had no choice but to keep pace. As they started down the wallaby trail Aaron heard the thud of hooves. The soldiers had mounted their horses and gone in the other direction in search of Lawrie and Paddy. He sighed and hoped they'd get away.

~

Chapter Twenty

Wallis Plains Barracks

Mick and Aaron had been imprisoned in the Wallis Plains barracks for two days. They were still manacled and expected to be sent to Sydney for trial any day. Aaron suspected it was just a matter of waiting for one of the boats to come up from Newcastle. There'd been no sign of the soldiers who were out searching for Paddy and Lawrie. Aaron took that to be a good sign – they must still be eluding capture.

It was mid-afternoon when all hope and speculation came to an end. Corporal Higgins arrived, along with two of the soldiers who'd been out searching. They had Paddy and Lawrie in custody. They were manacled and Lawrie had what was left of a bloody shirt wrapped around his right hand. They shoved them roughly into the cell and locked the door behind them.

"What happened? How'd you get caught?" asked Aaron eager for news of their brief bid for freedom.

"After they caught Mick we got away well an' good," said Paddy, "we got caught by a couple of fencers as we were passing through Duguid's."

"Aye," put in Lawrie. "They were only ter happy ter hand us over."

"Damn," said Mick frowning. "I was sure ye'd get away."

Paddy shrugged. "Have they told yer what they intend ter do with us?"

"No," replied Aaron. "I expect they'll send us to Sydney for trial. They'll want a public hanging for sure." He was still surprised at himself. He felt so calm talking about being hung. He wondered briefly if something was wrong with him.

"How's yer hand?" asked Mick grimacing at the bloody shirt wrapped around Lawrie's hand.

"Completely buggered," said Lawrie looking at it. "It's got shit stuck in it an' I can hardly move it. And it hurts like hell."

Aaron swallowed and grimaced. Lawrie would likely lose the use of it if they didn't get the shrapnel out. Not that it would matter soon either way. He, like the rest of them, would be dead.

"Do yer know what they did with Riley?" asked Paddy changing the subject.

Aaron shook his head.

"He was still lyin' in the dirt when we left," said Mick.

"Shit. Poor bugger," said Lawrie.

He'd been close to Riley. In fact, Aaron was sure he'd not only admired him but considered him to be a bit of a hero. Lawrie would no doubt take his death the hardest.

Two days later the boat arrived from Newcastle. The four of them were chained together before being taken down to the pier under the watchful eye of Corporal Higgins and three Privates. Once onboard they were secured in a small cell in the hold. It was stuffy and cramped, with barely enough room for the four of them to lie down. The ceiling was so low that none of them could stand up, and they spent the next twelve hours squashed up against one another. They were under constant guard. Corporal Higgins was taking no chances and had accompanied them along with the three Privates.

It was an overnight trip down the river to Newcastle, and they docked at the wharf at first light. As soon as they emerged from the hold Aaron sucked in a deep breath of air. It had been suffocating in the hold of the small riverboat. It had reminded him of being on the hulk in Brazil. He'd been imprisoned on it for three months while repairs were made to the ship. It had been hot, humid and airless. The small hold on the riverboat brought back that same feeling of being smothered, of not being able to get enough air into his lungs. He took in another deep breath as they shuffled down the gangplank. The air was ripe with the smell of rotting fish, and he screwed up his face.

Corporal Higgins ushered them along the wharf to a larger vessel which would take them to Sydney. Aaron shuffled along as best he could. Being chained to the others made it impossible to walk any faster. He remembered the first time he'd worn leg irons, and how he'd walked with an odd gait until he got used to them. He was walking a bit like that now.

It was only a short walk along the wharf to board the ship bound for Sydney. The Newcastle docks catered for the riverboats and coastal vessels that plied the waters between here and Sydney. The larger ships generally didn't come into the port and so the wharf was relatively small, with only enough berths for a half dozen ships to dock at once.

They boarded the cutter Sophia and were immediately led down into the hold. There were several holding cells which were large enough to hold a dozen or so men. They were locked in one of them and two of the Privates were posted to guard them. They were still chained together and so they were forced to all sit on the one bunk. Aaron sighed. They would be in Sydney in a few hours, and then what? Would they be tried immediately? He thought so. He wondered if Tom and John had been tried and if they'd been sentenced to hang.

The ship didn't set sail for Sydney until that evening. By then Aaron was feeling so cramped and uncomfortable, and he was sure the others were as well. They'd been chained together since yesterday morning, and it was impossible to find a comfortable position for any length of time. Lawrie was in terrible pain with his hand, and he was looking pale and gaunt. Aaron let out his breath slowly and tried to think of something other than the cramp in his arms.

~

The Sophia docked in Sydney early the following morning and the four men were immediately taken to the Sydney Gaol in George Street. The gaol was an imposing brick building with the gallows towering above its walls. Aaron shuddered as he entered through the large gates. The sight of the gallows had awoken the serpent of fear in his belly. It squirmed and writhed and he thought he might be sick.

They were immediately taken to one of the cells and much to Aaron's relief were unchained from one another, although the manacles remained. The cell was about twelve feet by twelve feet and had a barred window set high in the wall. It contained two cribs and four hammocks which were strung above the cribs. It was already occupied. Two men looked up as the door swung open and the four of them were shoved inside.

"Paddy, Lawrie. Oh my God ye got caught," said Tom Moss jumping to his feet at the sight of them.

"We were hoping you'd got away," said John O'Donnell rising from the crib.

"Aye so were we. But we thought yer two would've been sentenced already," said Paddy grinning at them.

"Aye, well we've been expectin' to be tried an' hanged, but it hasn't happened yet," said Tom sitting back down on the nearest crib. "Perhaps it will now."

Aaron nodded. He thought Tom was right. They'd probably been waiting until they had them all in custody and could try them together. In that case, they'd all hang for sure.

"Well we're hoping not ter hang," said John casting an odd look at Tom. "If the good Lieutenant comes through as he promised."

"What are yer talking about?" said Paddy, confusion evident on his face.

Tom looked sheepish. "Aye well I gave some information to Hicks, an' he promised to put in a good word for us with the Magistrate."

"Yer snitched on us?" said Paddy anger blazing in his eyes. His temper was never far from the surface and from the look on his face, it was about to explode.

"Yer told him about Tom Boardman didn't yer?" said Lawrie glaring at him.

Paddy rolled his hand into a fist and hit Tom square in the face. It made an awful cracking sound as made contact with his nose. Tom was knocked sideways into the wall, with blood spurting from his broken nose. Paddy drew his arm back ready to land another blow when Aaron grabbed him.

"Stop. If the guards come you'll get a flogging," he said holding him as tight as he could. He could feel his muscles flexing under his fingers and he gripped him as hard as he could. "He's not worth it."

Paddy was breathing heavily and struggling against Aaron. Mick grabbed him on the other side and between the two of them they restrained him from hitting Tom a second time.

"Yer a fuckin' little arsehole," he said and he spat at him.

"Come on mate," said Mick straining to hold him. "Aaron's right. He ain't worth a floggin'."

Paddy was still breathing heavily, but Aaron felt his muscles slowly relax under his fingers. He glanced at Mick, who nodded and they cautiously let him go. The anger hadn't completely left him, but he seemed to have himself under control. He sucked in several large breaths and turned away from Tom who was still in the corner of the crib holding his face. If he were Tom he'd be staying as far away from Paddy as he could.

The atmosphere in the confined cell was tense as Paddy and Lawrie continued to glare at Tom. Aaron hoped they'd be able to keep them apart. He wasn't sure if Paddy was going take to him again or not. He was currently pacing up and down breathing heavily. Every so often he'd stop and glare at Tom. If Lawrie's hand wasn't injured he'd probably take to Tom as well. He sighed. Tom had been an idiot to trust

Hicks, but it was too late now, the damage was done.

Paddy had only just stopped pacing and sat down on one of the cribs when a guard appeared at their cell accompanied by a Reverend. He was a middle-aged portly man but otherwise rather nondescript. He was wearing metal-rimmed spectacles, but even behind them, Aaron could see kindness in his watery blue eyes. Not that he had much time for men of God, and he doubted the others would require his services.

The guard unlocked the cell and the Reverend stepped inside. He immediately spied Lawrie and smiled kindly at him.

"I'm Reverend George Bennett, the gaol's Chaplain," he said. "I heard there was a man with a badly injured hand just brought in. Come with me and we'll ask the surgeon to take a look at it."

Lawrie looked wary and glanced from the Reverend to the others as if he was seeking their support. Aaron knew he was in awful pain, so he gave him a nod and glanced towards the Reverend.

"You should go with him."

"Thank yer," said Lawrie getting to his feet.

Reverend Bennett gestured for him to walk ahead of him out of the cell. He then turned his attention to Tom who was still cowering at the back of the crib. His nose was broken and his face was already showing signs of bruising and swelling.

"Perhaps you should come as well," he said smiling kindly at Tom. "I'm sure the surgeon won't mind if I bring him two patients instead of one."

Tom looked nervously around the small cell. "No, I'm fine thank ye."

"If you're sure."

"Aye, I am."

"Alright I won't press you," he said and followed Lawrie from the cell.

Aaron breathed a sigh of relief. It would only cause more trouble if Tom made a fuss or told the guards what happened. However, he was glad that Lawrie was having his hand attended to. He couldn't imagine what pain he must be in.

~

Weeks went by and still, there was no word of when they might be tried. Aaron couldn't help thinking that they'd forgotten about them. Of course, he knew they hadn't. It was obviously taking a while for the court to gather all the evidence against them. He just wanted it over and done with.

The situation between Tom and John and the others hadn't improved. Paddy would give Tom a shove and glare at him if he came anywhere near him. And it was difficult not to in the small cramped cell. Aaron and Mick were doing their utmost to keep them apart and maintain the peace. Aaron wasn't sure how much longer that would last before Paddy exploded again.

It was nearing midday when the gaoler arrived at their cell with four soldiers.

"Stand aside," he said as he unlocked their cell door and swung it open.

Aaron and the others stood back and two of the soldiers entered. One of them had several lengths of chain with him.

"Put your hands out," he said to Aaron who was nearest him. He did as he was bid and he attached one end of the chain to his manacles. He then attached the other end to Lawrie before chaining Lawrie to Paddy. He continued until they were all chained one to the other.

"What's going on?" asked Paddy as they were being marched out of the cell.

"Keep moving," he said giving Tom a shove. "You're standin' trial today."

At those words, Aaron felt his stomach do a somersault. He sucked in a breath and swallowed as he tried to regain control of his nerves. He knew this day would come, and he was prepared for it. At least he thought he was. This wasn't his first trial, and he well remembered how he felt last time he was sentenced to hang. Again, a pang of fear surged through his belly.

Following the sentencing, a numbness had settled itself in his bones, and everything seemed to be happening from a distance - like he was down the end of a long tunnel. Perhaps he was already dead? But no that would be too much to ask for.

Every time he'd heard the gaoler coming he expected him to stop at their cell. Well, tis time. They'll be hangin' ye today. But no. He always kept on going and Aaron went back into his self-made cocoon where he was safe from the world. He hated the waiting. Not knowing when they would hang him was torture. James was no company either. He'd withdrawn into himself and merely grunted if Aaron spoke to him.

Aaron didn't know how long it'd been since they'd been sentenced. He'd lost all track of time, but he expected every day would be his last. He heard the jangle of the gaoler's keys, and by the sound of the footsteps on the stone floor, he wasn't alone. He sat up and peered into the gloom straining to see who was coming. His heart began thumping harder as he imagined the soldiers that would be with the gaoler – today would be the day.

The gaoler stopped outside their cell and unlocked the door. Aaron was surprised to see a well-dressed man illuminated by the gaoler's lantern. He'd been expecting soldiers assigned to escort them to the gallows.

"Aaron Price and James Barton?" he queried in a cultured London accent.

"Aye," said Aaron cautiously. He had no idea what this man would have to do with them.

"I'm Sir John Richardson, Knight of the Justices," he said peering at them. "I'm here to inform you that you've both been given a reprieve from the Court of Common Pleas at Westminster."

Aaron looked at James who shrugged and then stared at the man. A reprieve? Did that mean what he thought it meant?

"A reprieve?" he asked, still not sure that he'd understood.

"That's right," said Sir John. "The death sentence has been revoked. You're to be transported for life to the colonies. In a few days, you'll be transferred to one of the prison hulks to await transportation." He gave them one final glance and left. "Good day."

Aaron stared after the man as the gaoler locked their cell door and continued down the corridor. He couldn't help the feeling of hope that washed over him. He wasn't going to die, and it was like a drab grey cloud had been lifted and the world was bathed in colour.

"James! Can you believe it!" he said turning to his dearest friend.

James has hunched over sobbing. Aaron breathed deeply and sat down beside him. He put his arm about his shoulders and the two of them sat there in silence. Exiled to the colonies was more than either of them could've hoped for.

Aaron pressed his lips together and breathed in through his nose. Well, that had been then, and he couldn't hope for anything other than hanging this time. He followed the two soldiers ahead of him out of the gaol and down the street to the courthouse. It was a warm day and the air smelled fresh compared to the stale odours of the gaol. It would be all over soon enough and he welcomed it. He wanted it over. He'd thrown his lot in with the mad Irishmen, and now he would pay the price for it.

~

Chapter Twenty One

Sydney, December 1825

It was cool in the courthouse. Once they'd gone up the steps and through the doors, the heat of the day was left behind. Two large cedar doors at the end of a wide tiled hallway were open, and the soldiers led them straight into the courtroom. It was an impressive room with its marble floor and cedar lined walls. The Chief Justice was seated at a large bench at one end of the room, and the jury of twelve were seated opposite. They watched them as they walked across the floor to the dock.

Aaron wondered if they'd attained some level of notoriety. By the looks some of the jurors were giving them he thought their infamy may have spread as far as Sydney. He knew they'd instilled fear into some of the settlers, particularly after burning Reid's house. Then there was the reward that Alexander Sharp had offered for their capture. He smirked as he gazed at the jurors across the other side of the room.

A small bespectacled man, who Aaron hadn't noticed until now, stood up and read from a sheet of parchment.

"The evidence against the accused has been presented and heard," he said in a clear voice. "Thomas Moss, John O'Donnell, Aaron Price, Lawrence Cleary, Patrick Clinch and Michael Cassidy are charged with larceny and burglary." He sat back down again.

"Have you the jurors reached a decision?" asked the Chief Justice.

Aaron glanced sideways at the others. Their faces remained passive and he wondered if this was what they'd expected. He'd thought they'd be in court to hear the evidence against them, but clearly not. This was a sentencing hearing – the decision of their guilt or innocence had already been made. He sighed and shrugged. Really it made little difference.

"We have your Honor," said a tall well-dressed man standing up. "We find the accused guilty as charged, and recommend the penalty of death."

"Thank you," said the Chief Justice before turning to face the prisoners. "Considering the nature of your crimes I do not feel compelled to recommend the Acting Governor reduce the sentence that I am about to pass." He paused and glanced down at the document he had in front of him. "Due to some mitigating evidence, I sentence John O'Donnell and Thomas Moss to transportation to Norfolk Island for life. Michael Cassidy is sentenced to transportation to Moreton Bay for life. As for Lawrence Cleary, Aaron Price and Patrick Clinch there can be only one sentence. You are sentenced to death by hanging."

Aaron wasn't surprised at the sentence, he'd expected to hang. The fear that he'd felt a few weeks ago when he'd seen the gallows remained dormant. He didn't feel much at all except rising anger that Hicks had come through for Tom and John and saved them from the gallows. He didn't dare look at Paddy. He would no doubt be furious. He wasn't sure he'd be able to stop him from hitting Tom again – he wasn't sure he wanted to. He'd like to hit him as well. Actually, he'd like nothing better than to sink his fist into something, and Tom would do nicely.

The soldiers ushered them out of the courtroom and back down the street to the gaol. The gallows loomed ominously above the walls and Aaron eyed them with a sense of impending destiny. He shied away from the thoughts of his future liaison with the hangman's noose, but he did wonder when it might be. Surely they would do it quickly. The waiting would be the worst.

The following morning two soldiers arrived at their cell and took Mick with them. Aaron hoped they'd come for Tom and John soon as well. Paddy and Lawrie had both been furious that their betrayal had been rewarded. Aaron agreed with them but had no intention of giving the guards any excuse to deliver their own form of punishment.

Anyway, Aaron thought Tom was in enough pain with his broken nose. He had two black eyes and half his face was swollen. He was also making an odd whistling noise every time he breathed in. The guards had questioned him about how he came to be in such a state, and Aaron was relieved that he hadn't blamed Paddy. That would have made the entire situation a hundred times worse.

It was just after midday when four more soldiers arrived with the guard. Oh good, they've come for John and Tom. Aaron would be glad to see them go.

"Lawrence Cleary, Aaron Price and Patrick Clinch," said a tall Private. "Ye to come with us."

Aaron sucked in a deep breath. Shit. He hadn't expected them to come for them so soon. He was ready, although the nervous flutter through his belly belied this. He followed Lawrie and Paddy out of the cell and down the hall behind the soldiers. He tried not to think. He didn't want to feel, didn't want to be in his own body right now. He expected them to exit through the doors at the end of the hallway which would take them out to the courtyard. Steps led up to gallows from there.

He was surprised when they showed them into another cell instead. It was a small cell with four cribs, a keg of water and a slops bucket. Two wooden chairs were against the back wall which also had a small barred window. They locked the door behind them and left.

"I thought they we're gonna hang us right now," said Lawrie looking alarmed. "I wasn't ready."

"Aye me neither," said Paddy sitting down on one of the chairs. "But I thought it was about ter happen."

Aaron shrugged. "I would've preferred it. I hate the waiting."

"I'm not in any great hurry ter meet the hangman," said Lawrie shuddering. "I don't mind waitin'."

"Well I don't reckon it will be too long," said Aaron looking around the small cell. "I expect this is the cell for the condemned. And that's us."

"Yer are so full of comfortin' words," said Lawrie frowning at him.

~

The following morning the Reverend Bennett was let into their cell. He was the gaol's chaplain and had been instrumental in having the surgeon treat Lawrie's hand. He smiled benignly at them before seating himself on one of the chairs under the window.

"I'm here to offer you what comfort I can," he said smiling warmly at them. "Your execution has been scheduled for this afternoon, and I offer you the Lord's love and forgiveness."

Lawrie visibly swallowed and paled at the news. Paddy scowled at the Reverend but said nothing. Aaron felt nothing but relief. Thank God he wouldn't have to wait much longer for this to be all over.

"Perhaps a prayer will help you to connect with God at this hour," he said, and not waiting for a reply bowed his head and commenced praying aloud. He spoke of God's love for all his children, and of forgiveness.

Aaron closed his eyes and bowed his head and allowed the Reverend's words to wash over him. They gave him neither solace nor hope. All he could think of was that he and God had never seen eye to eye, and he didn't expect that to change now. He raised his head and opened his eyes when the Reverend's prayer ended. A quick glance at Paddy and Lawrie told him that the Reverend's words had not had any effect on them either.

"No amount of praying will make any difference now," said Aaron. His voice was flat and emotionless. "Save your words for those that appreciate them."

Reverend Bennett smiled and nodded, but remained seated under the window. "Perhaps words are not necessary," he said smiling at them. "I will stay until they come for you."

Lawrie seemed comforted by the Reverend's presence, but Paddy glared at him.

"Please yerself," said Paddy.

They sat in silence. Each man no doubt consumed by their own thoughts on their impending execution. For Aaron, it was like the events of the past few years had been building to this moment. From the instant, he'd agreed to break into Robinson's house his life had been put on this course – and now it had come to an end. An end he could almost taste and welcomed. At least that's what he was telling himself.

He hoped when the time came he still felt the same way.

The gaoler arrived with their midday meal. This would generally consist of some rice and peas or cheese and bread, but today it was a beef stew with dark bread. Aaron sopped up the gravy with a piece of bread and relished every bite. It would be his last meal, and it tasted better than anything he'd eaten in a while. When he'd finished he sat back on the narrow crib and sighed.

The Reverend sat quietly on the chair. He offered no further words of comfort or prayer, but his very presence was unnerving Aaron. He glanced at him. He was sitting there with his head bowed – probably in silent prayer. He was a plain middle-aged balding man, who exuded an air of calm and kindness. It was his calm demeanour that Aaron found so disconcerting.

They hadn't long finished their midday meal when the guard returned.

"Reverend I 'ave an urgent message for ye," he said sticking a piece of paper through the bars.

"Thank you," said Reverend Bennett getting to his feet and walking over to the door. He took the message from between his grubby fingers and smiled kindly at the guard. He sat back down on his chair by the window and unfolded the paper.

It took him a couple of minutes to read the long message, and Aaron couldn't help but wonder what sort of message could be so urgent and long-winded. He sighed and went back to trying to think of anything except when the soldiers would come for them. Thoughts of his family had been sneaking into his consciousness, but he didn't want to think about them either.

"Well gentlemen, we have a new Governor," said Reverend Bennett beaming at them. "Lieutenant General Ralph Darling was appointed to the position two days ago. That is wonderful news."

Paddy looked unimpressed and Lawrie stared at him. Why would they care who the new Governor was? Aaron was perplexed because the Reverend looked so damned pleased with the news.

"I'm sorry," he said looking at them with a more serious expression. "Of course you don't understand the significance of this news. The new Governor is inclined to leniency, and in good faith has reduced your sentence. He's revoked the sentence of death. You're to be transported to Norfolk Island."

The three of them fell to their knees in shock and surprise. Lawrie grabbed the hem of the Reverend's cloak and sobbed. Paddy was speechless. Aaron was furious. He was ready to die, had planned for it and readied himself. There were worse things than hanging. What the fuck were they going to do to him now?

He put his head in his hands and allowed the heart-wrenching sobs to escape. He wasn't sure if they were tears of relief or grief. The one thing he was certain of was that he'd have to face the future. Norfolk Island? He'd heard of it – hell on earth.

The End

What Became of the Jacob's Mob?

Patrick Clinch (Paddy)

He was sentenced to life on Norfolk Island. In 1827 he was murdered by a group of soldiers. Although charged with his murder, they were found to be not guilty of the crime.

Laurence Cleary (Lawrie)

He spent a short time on Norfolk Island before being transferred to Cockatoo Island. He was granted a Ticket of Leave in 1852 for the district of Port Phillip.

Thomas Moss (Tom)

He was sentenced to life on Norfolk Island. He was granted a Ticket of Leave for the district of Ilawarra, and given a Conditional Pardon in 1849,

Michael Cassidy (Mick)

He was sentenced to transportation to Moreton Bay, and was granted a Certificate of Freedom in May 1841.

John McDonnell (John)

He was sentenced to transportation to Norfolk Island. He was executed in 1832 for the attempted murder of fellow convict Thomas Smith.

Aaron Price (Aaron)

He was sentenced to transportation to Norfolk Island for life. He turned his life around, and took up several positions working for the Government. These included Police Runner and Overseer on the island. He was granted a Ticket of Leave in March 1838 and a Conditional Pardon in 1847. He remained on the island until its closure.

Author Notes

Thank you so much for reading my book. I'm an Australian indie author. As such, I maintain complete control of my work and self publish. That also means I have to market and promote my work, which I'm not very good at. I find it hard to self promote.

So, I'm taking this opportunity to not only thank you for taking the time to read my book, but if you liked it, would you mind leaving a rating or review on Amazon. It's the best way to show any author that you appreciate their hard work. It also helps other potential readers to decide if they should invest their time and money.

You already know that I write historical fiction, and you may have also realised that my stories are based on the lives of my ancestors. I've been passionate about family history for many years, and I've discovered so many amazing ancestors who led such interesting lives. So, I blend fact with fiction and bring their stories to life, and I'm so excited to be sharing them with you.

If you enjoyed this book, please consider reading one of my other titles.

Thank you

Pioneers of Burra

From Cornwall to an untamed South Australia...

Based on the true story of the Bryar family, who left their homeland in search of a better life. Richard and his son Thomas secure free passage to South Australia, where they dream of a new beginning working in the copper mine of Burra.

After months at sea and a perilous journey from Adelaide to Burra, their families are finally reunited. Can they overcome the hardships of living in a dugout on the Burra Creek to carve out a better future for their children? Will a disaster in the mine finally bring them together with hope for the future?

Margaret

From Bredgar House to Van Diemen's Land.....

Margaret Chambers never imagined she'd be forced to flee her family home and country to escape a hideous old man and an arranged marriage. Pretending to be a general servant she boards a ship bound for Hobart Town. It's 1837, and in order to get free passage out to Van Diemen's Land, she's agreed to work for Mrs Hector. There's just one problem, she's never done a day's menial work in her life and her lie is soon discovered.

Taken into the household of the Reverend Davies and his wife Maria, she not only finds kindness but friendship, and is employed as Maria's companion. She couldn't have hoped for a better situation, but when convict and scoundrel William Hartley crosses her path will it all come tumbling down? Seduced by the young and charming William she finds herself unable to remain with the Reverend and his wife. Maria doesn't want her to go but Margaret can see the conflict between Maria and her husband. Not wanting to be the cause of any rift between them she leaves.

William still has five years of his seven-year sentence to serve and he's not free to marry her. However, he stands by her side by stealing food for her and his unborn child until he gets caught. Sent away to work on the chain gang Margaret's left to fend for herself. Somehow she finds a way to survive until William's free to join her and when he gets a Ticket of Leave and permission to marry her, the future's looking hopeful.

Jacob's Mob

Printed in Great Britain
by Amazon